I0635347

TRANSPARENT MINDS IN
SCIENCE FICTION

Transparent Minds in Science Fiction

An Introduction to Accounts of Alien, AI and Post-Human Consciousness

Paul Matthews

https://www.openbookpublishers.com

©2023 Paul Matthews

All external links were active at the time of publication unless otherwise stated and have been archived via the Internet Archive Wayback Machine at https://archive.org/web

Digital material and resources associated with this volume are available at https://doi.org/10.11647/OBP.0348#resources

ISBN Paperback: 978-1-80511-046-0
ISBN Hardback: 978-1-80511-047-7
ISBN Digital (PDF): 978-1-80511-048-4
ISBN Digital ebook (epub): 978-1-80511-049-1
ISBN XML: 978-1-80511-051-4
ISBN HTML: 978-1-80511-052-1
DOI: 10.11647/OBP.0348

Cover image: NASA, Nebula, May 4, 2016. https://unsplash.com/photos/rTZW4f02zY8
Cover design: Jeevanjot Kaur Nagpal

For Caroline, Sam and James
Who supported and encouraged this work

Table of Contents

Preface

This book is based on two abiding sources of excitement and awe: the science of the brain and the stories of science fiction.

Ever since reading J Z Young's *Programs of the Brain* at school I have been intrigued by the brain and our slowly unfolding knowledge of how it works. Based as it was on the learning opportunities afforded by brain misfunction—due to injury or illusion—the research that *Programs of the Brain* described struck me as practical and evidence-based science, one benefiting in its explanatory power through the (then) new metaphor of the computer.

A key unsolved mystery of the brain is what gives rise to conscious experience and what purpose it serves. A multitude of possible answers have been made to these questions, some more evidence-based than others, some still using an underlying computing model and others breaking away from it. To some, the problem is insolvable. To others, it is not a problem at all and not worth focusing on any more. To most, it has certainly not been resolved in any satisfactory way.

Also early on I developed a love for collections of science fiction short stories stocked at the local library. Written in the creative explosion of the genre around the 1960s and 1970s, these stories were wonderful not only in their variety and idiosyncrasy, but also in their common profound optimism and unfettered thinking about what else could be, what alien worlds and psychological states might be possible. This affection for science fiction has continued into adulthood. Now, as a technologist, I frequently see references to how science fiction can both predict and shape what comes to be. Despite being speculative, its underpinnings in science fact help to unveil possible worlds that must contain fragments of truth. As the genre has developed from the 'rocket man' comic book derring do of the 1950s to the current incredible range of inter-weaved sub-genres, we see an increasing number of examples attempting to access the inner worlds of the characters and situations they describe. This diversification has been significantly improved by the increasing gender and cultural diversity of authors, bringing a rich variety of life experience and viewpoint to the genre. So I feel there is an opportunity to sift some of this work to see how it can help us to understand sentience and how it might extend to evolved alien and manufactured minds.

I feel that this is also timely, as there is a discussion over the likelihood (and risk) of sentience and free will in future AIs. At the same time, possibilities for human enhancement—through chemical means, through digital implants and interfaces, or direct thought communication between people—are becoming more real. So what kind of experience might this lead to in people and machines? I think fiction can be a great source of inspiration for this.

1. Introduction

> Literature is a record of human consciousness, the richest and most
> comprehensive we have... The novel is arguably (humanity's) most
> successful effort to describe the experience of individual human beings
> moving through space and time.
>
> David Lodge[1]

It should be more widely appreciated that literature is a kind of scientific
tool that can be used to shed light on consciousness. The argument is
that the richest description of the phenomenon of human experience
come from our finest writers, who are capable of capturing moments in
time in exquisite detail from multiple perspectives. In this view, there
is no need to argue that either science or the humanities represent true
knowledge, but that the two can complement one another productively,
the latter unveiling a personalised view that science—with its third
person fixation—cannot achieve.[2]

Science Fiction (SF) authors are often well versed in neuroscience
and philosophy and see their literature as thought experiments or
models of problems on far off, but feasible, technological horizons. As
Swirsky notes, SF is a model in multidisciplinary alignment: 'literature,
philosophy and science are, in my opinion, inseparable manifestations
of the same creative instinct that has operated throughout the ages.'[3]

---

1   David Lodge, *Consciousness and the Novel: Connected Essays* (Cambridge, MA:
    Harvard University Press, 2002), 10.
2   Philosophy has also been criticised for being limited in the same way. As Simon
    Glendinning points out, it is too coldly logical and argument-centred. He sees a
    clear role for imaginative literature that presents a compelling expression of mental
    states. Simon Glendinning, *In the Name of Phenomenology* (London: Routledge,
    2007).
3   Peter Swirski, *Between Literature and Science: Poe, Lem, and Explorations in Aesthetics,
    Cognitive Science, and Literary Knowledge* (Montreal: McGill-Queen's University
    Press, 2000), 139.

    https://doi.org/10.11647/OBP.0348.01

My thesis is that science fiction with a psycho-emotional flavour can provide new insight into both current human consciousness and also possible future states of consciousness in both ourselves and the machines we create. The reciprocal move is that inspiration for the artistic portrayal of these states can come from the science of our own world, which is still only gradually revealing causes for sentience in humans and other animals.

In the following pages, we will see examples of how SF authors approach this multidisciplinary alignment in their works. It is first worth introducing the narrative and literary theories that can help to explain both the authors' art and the readers' experience.

Psychonarration and monologue: backgrounding the author

Literature that includes characters' mental states has been around since as far back as the eighteenth century but reached a peak of sophistication in the early twentieth. The use of techniques such as psychonarration and monologue—where the viewpoint enters the characters' minds—powered the modernist approach to literature and enabled highly psychological writing. Authors such as Proust, Austen, Joyce and Woolf have been celebrated for their powerful insights into the experience of memory, emotion, motivation and consciousness. A large part of their innovation and craft was to move from the classic (external) narrative voice which could be intrusive and domineering, to ways of telling a story where the writer merges with the character so closely that they almost disappear. As Nelles suggests in his study of Jane Austen, in this way the novelist 'creates the impression that the reader has more or less direct access to the character's mind rather than through a firewall of narrative commentary.'[4]

In her classic analysis *Transparent Minds*, Dorrit Cohn groups these narrative techniques into third and first-person types and notes how some provide more authentic impressions of mind-reading, with third person psychonarration (incorporating the method of 'free indirect

---

4   William Nelles, 'Austen's Juvenilia and the Sciences of the Mind', in *Jane Austen and Sciences of the Mind*, ed. Beth Lau, 14–36 (London: Routledge, 2017), 18.

speech') the most effective followed by monologue. In these modes, dialogue is no longer visible by way of well-defined quotation marks, but mixes with the narrative. The author's own opinions or moralising can be reduced or removed entirely, with the result that we can more readily believe we are observing the accounts of individual personalities directly. Cohn explains how 'narrative fiction is the only literary genre, as well as the only kind of narrative, in which the unspoken thoughts, feelings and perceptions of a character other than the speaker can be portrayed.'[5]

Cohn notes the enormous challenge of trying to project into other minds. No wonder then, that attempting the same for non-human minds is something that relatively few SF authors have attempted.

Neuroaesthetics: fiction and the feeling of consciousness

When analysts have examined how these great writers achieve their effects, they have been able to link fictionally depicted states to scientific knowledge of those states. This approach, which seeks to combine literary criticism with relevant brain science, has been termed 'neuroaesthetics' by Kay Young. It is enacted via Young's principle of resonance, the way in which a book's language triggers the experience within with the reader: 'the principle of listening and looking for compelling resonances in language, meaning and representation (yielding) shared accounts of integrated mind.'[6] Young sees it as particularly important to maintain the emotional and embodied experience of reading when studying and experiencing texts from authors who write about mental states.

This reader-author dynamic is one way in which literature may provide more fertile imaginary ground than science. Philip Davis puts it thus: 'what literature does, which formal philosophy does not—and what literature can hardly help doing—is yield more than its writers know... writers offer this by creating not so much a line of argument

---

5   Dorrit Cohn, *Transparent Minds: Narrative Modes for Presenting Consciousness in Fiction* (Princeton, NJ: Princeton University Press, 1978), 7.
6   Kay Young, *Imagining Minds: The Neuro-Aesthetics of Austen, Eliot, and Hardy* (Columbus: Ohio State University Press, 2010), 10.

as a resonant space for thinking.'[7] So literature itself may be a cognitive extension.[8] Reading literature allows for first person, active insight and has a moral dimension—by making us feel directly addressed and immersed, it forces us to be involved. Famed science fiction author Ursula Le Guin is skilled at weaving together scientific knowledge with philosophical and ethical speculation using story:

> Science describes accurately from outside, poetry describes accurately from inside. Science explicates, poetry implicates. Both celebrate what they describe. We need the languages of both science and poetry to save us from merely stockpiling endless 'information' that fails to inform our ignorance or our irresponsibility.[9]

Here, Le Guin identifies the missed opportunity of the solely objective—the chance for readers to recognise themselves in the process of reading and to access their imaginations.

Consciousness from the outside and inside

Most approaches to consciousness in science and philosophy certainly *have* been on the objective side, seeing subjectivity as either unscientific, or a difficult-to-explain emergent property of the system. A leading paradigm in neuroscience-oriented theories of consciousness is not that it is fundamentally a different substance, but that it is explainable in terms of the neural material from which it arises (materialism). Several promising explanatory directions exist within materialism and include the need to have a unified, generally available picture of the current state (global workspace), the brain's capacity to combine multiple signals (integrated information), a spatially organised internal representation of the body (self-modelling) and the assumption of different levels of symbolic representation (with consciousness as a higher level, localised representation).

---

7   Philip Davis, *Reading and the Reader: The Literary Agenda* (Oxford: University Press, 2013), 4.

8   Davis notes neurological evidence that novel metaphors lead to more brain activity than do clichés. He goes on to quote Joseph Gold on the cognitive power of literature: 'Literature itself has become for both writers and readers 'a brain extension' which has added a new level of consciousness to human brains 'because by means of writing and reading the brain could feedback thought to itself", Ibid.

9   Ursula Le Guin, *Late in the Day: Poems 2010–2014* (Oakland, CA: PM Press, 2016), 7.

Some key principles are shared by these leading theories: the existence of the widely interconnected, yet modularised neuronal pathways in the different parts of the brain; the extent of internal feedback from signals to achieve changes in the external and internal world; and the overall complexity of the organisation of the brain itself. These factors combined may eventually yield a reliable test or universally accepted standard of consciousness.[10]

While materialist theories can perform well in explaining experimental findings and human performance and may all have elements of the overall picture, they remain unsatisfying in certain ways. The traditional stance of science and philosophy, exemplified by materialism, is external objectivity, yet this usually ignores or cannot deal with the view from within. A second movement, that of phenomenology, attempts to use conscious experience and structure as a method to access truth about the nature of the world. Phenomenology tries to bring science's rigour to the study of subjectivity, with a number of flavours differently emphasising embodiment and perception. This often led theorists to invent new language to describe the sense-world interface, such as Heidegger's *Dasein* (a conscious being) and the state of 'being-in-the-world' (unifying subject, object and consciousness).[11] This can make them relatively very hard to understand and they have been accused of not adding much of practical value. But phenomenology as a method—the deliberate and structured attention to, and description of, the lived experience—can add practically to our understanding of different people's viewpoints. It also fundamentally describes the work of authors when they are building fictional mental states.

---

10   Indeed, Christof Koch already proposes the 'zap and zip' test of consciousness in which a magnetic pulse is applied to the brain and the waves of ensuing perturbation are measured by an EEG. The complexity of the measured response boils down to a single 'zipped' number. The zap and zip response takes advantage of the same algorithm used for file compression, dubbed the perturbational complexity index (PCI). The PCI seems to represent consciousness levels quite well, both in human wakeful states and in people who are asleep or comatose. *The Feeling of Life Itself: Why Consciousness Is Widespread but Can't Be Computed* (Cambridge, MA: The MIT Press, 2019).

11   Michael Wheeler, 2020, 'Martin Heidegger', in *The Stanford Encyclopedia of Philosophy*, ed. Edward N. Zalta, Fall 2020. Metaphysics Research Lab, Stanford University. https://plato.stanford.edu/archives/fall2020/entries/heidegger/.

> Seeking the essence of consciousness… will consist in rediscovering my actual presence to myself, the fact of my consciousness… Looking for the world's essence is not looking for what it is as an idea once it has been reduced to a theme of discourse; it is looking for what it is as a fact to us, before any thematization.[12]

Phenomenology as an approach had a direct applicability to literature and the subjective insight brought about by reading. For Wolfgang Iser, the 'blanks' or 'gaps' in more difficult or experimental fictional texts are what gives rise to a deeper experience of the readers' own consciousness and a purer experience of the world: 'It gives rise to a mode of communication through which the openness of the world is transferred in its very openness into the reader's conscious mind.'[13]

In the case of consciousness, science's 'view from nowhere' may have been a real limiting factor in the development of theory. Leading neuroscientists with a materialist orientation—such as Koch—have admitted this, saying all we can really start with is our own conscious experience and progress from there. This admission of the unavoidable need for some subjectivity feels like progress, as does the admission that the kind of experience we have cannot be solely claimed by the human species.[14] Koch has been vocal in attributing forms of consciousness to both lower and higher animals and the approach to an explanation of consciousness that he espouses—integrated information theory—can be applied to silicon brains and even some inanimate objects as much as human grey matter. This kind of thinking is taken to a logical conclusion in the theory of panpsychism (not widely accepted!), that everything in the world may have some level of consciousness.[15]

---

12 Maurice Merleau-Ponty, *The Phenomenology of Perception*, ed. Thomas Baldwin (London: Routledge, 2003), 72.

13 Wolfgang Iser, *The Act of Reading: A Theory of Aesthetic Response* (Baltimore: The Johns Hopkins University Press, 1978), 211.

14 Christof Koch, *The Feeling of Life Itself: Why Consciousness Is Widespread but Can't Be Computed* (Cambridge, MA: The MIT Press, 2019), 26.

15 Philip Goff, William Seager, and Sean Allen-Hermanson, 'Panpsychism', in *The Stanford Encyclopedia of Philosophy*, ed. Edward N. Zalta, Summer 2022. Metaphysics Research Lab, Stanford University. https://plato.stanford.edu/archives/sum2022/entries/panpsychism/.

Approaching the alien

While it is certainly difficult enough to describe our own conscious experience, how much more difficult it is to imagine and describe this kind of experience in non-human minds? This further removal needs an enormous amount of creativity and is to some extent constrained by language. In 'What Is It Like to Be a Bat?', the philosopher Thomas Nagel concludes that bats probably have a form of consciousness, but that it is likely to elude our ability to understand and explain it:

> Bats, although more closely related to us than those other species, nevertheless present a range of activity and a sensory apparatus so different from ours that the problem I want to pose is exceptionally vivid... anyone who has spent some time in an enclosed space with an excited bat knows what it is to encounter a fundamentally alien form of life.[16]

Nagel goes on to compare the alienness of other animal species to 'actual' aliens: 'And if there is conscious life elsewhere in the universe, it is likely that some of it will not be describable even in the most general experiential terms available to us.'[17] Generally speaking, for Nagel, the inner life of alien minds is even harder to approach than that of fellow animals with some shared sensory world: 'The more different from oneself the other experiencer is, the less success one can expect with this enterprise.'[18]

As we will see later on, science fiction works such as those of Stanislaw Lem depict alien intelligence so different from human intelligence that communication—at least in the way we understand it—is impossible. Any theory of mind that can be formed by the humans in these stories is depicted as being embarrassingly inadequate.

Nagel's thought experiment is bolstered by the concept of *umwelt*, the idea that the subjective universe of humans and other animals must vary enormously due to their different sensory apparatus, cognitive limitations and motivations.

---

16   Thomas Nagel 'What Is It Like to Be a Bat?', *The Philosophical Review* 83, no. 4 (1974): 438. https://doi.org/10.2307/2183914.

17   Ibid., 439.

18   Ibid., 442.

Humans often mistakenly assume that the *umwelt* they experience reflects the totality of the objective universe, the 'world out there', whereas in reality, the human *umwelt* only captures a small portion of what may be objectively (and physically) experienced by another species.

Although Nagel seems fairly pessimistic about this problem being resolved logically, he does admit that imagination is one way that it can be approached. This leap of imagination might not address the felt need to describe consciousness in objective terms, but it can take a step closer to what might be the imagined subjective world of different beings.

And we may not need to solely rely on the abstract. People *can* learn to echolocate by using sound to detect objects, albeit in a less sophisticated way than bats. Some blind people can use this to navigate, and may become so proficient that they describe the experience as analogous to *seeing* the world. This illustrates the brain's remarkable plasticity in adapting to new kinds of input, when paired with a data stream can be trained by trial and error to become effectively new senses (and similar brain areas to those that deal with vision, hearing etc. are adapted to this purpose).

The genre of Science Fiction

History and Subgenres

The literary theorists quoted at the beginning of this introduction, who propound a cognitive approach to criticism, tend to concentrate their focus on established 'high' literature to illustrate examples of how great writing can invoke mental states. I want to bring the same approach using science fiction sources, though in doing so need to admit that the genre has not always had a reputation for producing great works approaching the type of critical acclaim traditionally reserved for literary canon. This has in part been attributed to the plethora of amateur and hobbyist writers who entered the genre in the middle to late twentieth century, fuelled by the ease of publishing in SF periodicals and anthologies and the general demand amongst the reading public for man-meets-alien fantasy adventures. But I would argue that, amongst this work and well into the present day, there really is a rich vein of highly innovative, thought provoking and powerful writing. Here I will briefly outline the history, diversity and methodology of the SF genre.

SF has been famously defined by Darko Suvin as 'a literary genre whose necessary and sufficient conditions are the presence and interaction of estrangement and cognition, and whose main device is an imaginative framework alternative to the author's empirical environment.'[19]

With its origins in Gothic fiction and mystery of the nineteenth century and earlier, science fiction was spurred by the rapid technological development and existential threat of war in the early part of the twentieth century, which saw classics such as HG Wells' *The War of the Worlds*. In addition, with the development of space exploration in the middle part of the previous century, an explosion of speculation occurred around what interplanetary and interstellar exploration might bring and what other life might exist in the universe. The optimism and exploratory zeal of these 'golden age' periods in part echoed the West's attitude to the concept of empire—that foreign lands exist to be discovered, claimed, and the natives quelled. Thereafter, coincident with the gradual contraction of empire and a youth rebellion, science fiction's 'new wave' of the 1960's often took an inward turn, focusing rather more on the unwelcome invasion of mother Earth by alien races intent on our extinction.[20] The end result of this move was SF's move to the psychological, with more stories playing out as much on the mental as the physical plane. Today, the genre is mature and widely varied, with many subgenres and genre mash-ups. Globalisation has led to more cultural cross-pollination, and the diversity of authors has increased markedly. As we will see, the increasing possibility of an AI-dominant future led to the growing theme of the singularity, or superhuman intelligences. More recently too, climate change and biodiversity loss have led to the emergence of Solar Punk where alternative futures, both pessimistic and optimistic, are imagined.

In one widely used, though far from neat subdivision of the science fiction genre, there is a spectrum from hard SF at one end, where the science is foregrounded, central to the story, reality-based and well

---

19   Darko Suvin, *Metamorphoses in Science Fiction: On the Poetics and History of a Literary Genre* (New Haven, CT: Yale University Press, 1979), 27.

20   Damian Broderick, 'New Wave and Backwash: 1960–1980', in *The Cambridge Companion to Science Fiction*, eds Edward James and Farah Mendlesohn (Cambridge: Cambridge University Press, 2003), 48.

researched, through space opera, where the stories are more formulaic, melodramatic adventures set in other worlds, to fantasy at the other end, where there is less regard to possibility.[21] Of course, this kind of over-generalisation masks the huge variety of approaches and styles. Many readers and publishers take an inclusive approach and these days, as the label SF (constantly in an apparent crisis of self-definition) is often applied to works which, on the surface at least, have a very different focus or setting than the more familiar space adventure. Such speculative fiction, as some prefer to call it, no longer fits on a simplistic scale of hard to soft, and may be more willing to introduce the fantastical.

Methodology

Indeed, some of the more powerful work achieves its effect through highly familiar stories and settings with only small, or gradually introduced weirdness. Successful fantasy, according to Forster, does not need to fully embrace the supernatural, but can merely suggest it or imply it through realistic sounding events where the supernatural seems to be lurking on the margins. Technically it often 'merges the kingdoms of magic and common sense by using words that apply to both, and the mixture (thus) created comes alive.'[22]

A shared technical vocabulary between author and reader certainly helps SF to achieve literary impact. Assuming scientific awareness amongst readers provides authors with the ability to refer to contemporary terms and theories and to also—through the knowledge that the scientific paradigm will often shift—extend the contemporary into possible, unrecognisable futures. This recognition of the ephemerality of scientific knowledge at any one time may be a root of science fiction's frequent attraction toward either optimistic or pessimistic futures. This constant churn of scientific theory has been dubbed the 'pessimistic induction' by philosophers of science. The argument is that when our theories about the world have changed so radically over the generations, they can't be accepted as wholly true at any one time.

---

21 This hard SF-fantasy continuum has been mapped by Roberts in developmental origins to Protestant rationalist—Catholic theology/magic and mysticism. Adam Charles Roberts, *The History of Science Fiction*, 2nd ed. (London: Palgrave Macmillan, 2016), 3.

22 E. M. Forster *Aspects of the Novel* (Harmondsworth: Penguin Books, 1962), 109.

Imagination makes possible a conceptual blending that combines existing concepts in new, unforeseen ways—a 'recombinatory metaphoric process', as cognitive linguists have called it (though perhaps necessarily limited by the available pool of proto-concepts).[23] In fact, imagination might be what we do all the time when we are not engaged in a specific activity. Alan Richardson ties imagination to the 'default mode network' functioning of the mind at rest, which alternates between memory, planning, navigation, emotional processing and theory of mind.[24]

The imaginative leap needed to enter alien 'heads' requires huge empathy and creativity on the part of both the reader and author in order to transcend most human constraints and experience. But there are perhaps some shared universal constraints, in that we can often assume shared laws of physics (though many now think that other universes may have a quite different physics). Still, this is a much harder task than writing in the first or third (human) person and requires very careful and innovative use of language, as referents and connotations may be very different than those shared by humans. As speculation gets further from grounded concepts and known linguistic norms, it becomes harder for reader and author to share meaning. We do have a head start, as we have the 'theory of mind' needed to infer the inner states of fellow humans by observing their actions and listening to their words.[25] For alien and artificial minds, we just need to go further. In this book I will bring together what I consider to be some fine examples of different authors' attempts to do just this. My hope is that you bring all your empathic power to the reading of their work. But let us first further explore what these authors have revealed of their technique for writing the mind.

---

23 Alan Cruse and William Croft, eds, 'Metaphor', in *Cognitive Linguistics*, 193–222. Cambridge Textbooks in Linguistics (Cambridge: Cambridge University Press, 2004). https://doi.org/10.1017/CBO9780511803864.009.

24 Indeed, theory of mind—our insights into the minds, motivations and feelings of others—has been extensively related to science fiction in Nicholas Pagan's *Theory of Mind and Science Fiction* (New York: Palgrave, 2014). https://doi.org/10.1057/9781137399120.0001 Using characters from *Frankenstein* to *Do Androids Dream Electric Sheep?*, Pagan places his examples along a spectrum from the 'low road' of shallow emotional empathy to the 'high road' of a more intellectual understanding of alien and synthetic minds. He concludes that science fiction should be taken seriously as a literary genre for its depth of insight into these phenomena.

25 Ibid.

2. Authorial Approaches

'Science' implies the world of fact and what we all agree on seems to be true in the natural world. 'Fiction' implies values and meanings, the stories we tell to make sense of things. David Hume argued that it's impossible to argue from the way the world is to the way the world ought to be and yet here is a genre that claims to be a kind of 'fact-values' reconciliation, a bridge between the two.

Kim Stanley Robinson[1]

How do our SF authors approach their work? How do they tackle the essential problem of the aesthetics of other minds, choose narrative modes and connect facts to values and meanings as Robinson describes? Fortunately, they have been generous enough to share aspects of their method and we can start to piece together some common themes, despite the natural variety in their styles. For instance, they have carefully chosen the narrative voice that fits the main consciousnesses they want to feature. They endeavour to portray the nonhuman despite the human constraints and reference points they have to work with. They decide how much detail to give the reader and how much to leave out, in order to build more reader involvement. Their own relation to the SF genre may vary enormously. But as we would expect, all the authors are abreast of developments across the sciences—how things are—in order to have a healthy wellspring of ideas as to how things could be.

Influences and inspiration

Of course, contemporary science is a pivotal influence on many of the writers quoted in this book, from physics through biology to brain

---

1   Kim Stanley Robinson, quoted in Richard Lea, 'Science Fiction: The Realism of the 21st Century', *The Guardian*, August 7, 2015.

          https://doi.org/10.11647/OBP.0348.02

science. Multi-award winning author of the *Imperial Radch* trilogy Ann Leckie notes the influence of reading about consciousness effects in split-brain patients and other effects of brain damage in order to develop her approach to portraying a ship-mind.[2] A further prolific and successful contemporary writer, Adrian Tchaikovsky, is surely not alone in keeping an ongoing dialogue with scientist friends and colleagues to sense-check his ideas about enhanced animals, alien consciousness and the joining of minds. He particularly notes the influence of Peter Godfrey-Smith's *Other Minds* on his development of octopus society and consciousness in *Children of Ruin*.[3] And scientists have helped to bridge the gap in highlighting the possibilities for forms of life as inspired by known biology and the range of conditions in which life is found on earth. Author Greg Egan notes the influence of Jack Cohen and Ian Stewart's *What does a Martian Look Like?*, a book on xenobiology that gathers together scientific knowledge of relevance to possible alien life.[4]

The extent of scholarship in the background research of these SF authors should not be underestimated. Kazuo Ishiguro reportedly spends up to five years in research, before developing a first draft.[5] Roger Zelazny once described his process to develop a sound scientific knowledge base:

> I sat down and made a list of everything I felt I should know more about. Astrophysics, Oceanography, Marine Biology, Genetics. Then when I'd finished the list I read one book in each of these areas. When I'd finished I went back and read a second book until I'd read ten books in each area. I thought that it wouldn't turn me into a terrific, fantastic expert but I'd at least have enough material there to know if I was saying something wrong.[6]

2   Ibid.
3   Sarah Lewin, 'Alien Minds, Alien Tech (and Spiders, Too): Q&A With Sci-Fi Author Adrian Tchaikovsky', Space.com, 15 May 2019. https://www.space.com/children-of-ruin-adrian-tchaikovsky.html.
4   Jack Cohen and Ian Stewart, *What Does a Martian Look Like?: The Science of Extraterrestrial Life* (London: Ebury Press, 2004).
5   Allardice, Lisa, 'Kazuo Ishiguro, 'AI, Gene-Editing, Big Data... I Worry We Are Not in Control of These Things Any More', *The Guardian*, 20 February 2021. https://www.theguardian.com/books/2021/feb/20/kazuo-ishiguro-klara-and-the-sun-interview.
6   Roger Zelazny, 'Zelazny & Amber—Phlog44 RZ Interview', interview by Alex Heatley, 1995. http://www.roger-zelazny.com/repository/phlogiston_interview.html.

Alongside such broad-based research, authors may then drill down on particular examples of species or phenomena to draw inspiration. Becky Chambers describes how her fictional worlds start with a consideration of basic functions of her aliens who are inspired by Earth zoology:

> With alien species, I start with biology. The Aandrisks, for example, are a reptile-like, ectothermic species who lay eggs. So how does that affect your architecture, or your concept of parenthood, or family, or the typical composition of a household? From there, I ask questions about how these things affect art and culture and government and philosophy and so on.[7]

A single powerful psychological and philosophical idea can also drive stories, as we see for example with zombies in Peter Watts' *Blindsight*, which plays on the philosophical thought experiment of other people being identical in all ways but not being conscious[8] In this vein, in Theodore Sturgeon's classic novel *More than Human*, children with diverse supernatural abilities can fuse consciousness. Sturgeon describes how the psychological idea of the 'gestalt', the central idea in the book, has been powerful and lasting both for him and his readers:

> The Gestalt relationship is something that people really and truly want to know. The Gestalt relationship has preoccupied me for so long—the concept of a whole entity made up of very discrete individuals who don't lose their individuality. Gestalt between people is not like an army or a fascist dictatorship where everybody does what he's told. It's not an idea or particular creed that people have or share. It's what they are.[9]

And while specific scientific knowledge has been a rich source of influence and inspiration, the realisation that science also reveals our own finite limits has been another. We will see how alternative senses and the power of neuroplasticity has been a strong influence on authors

---

7   Becky Chambers, quoted in Ann Leckie, Kim Stanley Robinson, and M John Harrison, 'If the Aliens Lay Eggs, How Does that Affect Architecture?': Sci-Fi Writers on How They Build Their Worlds', *The Guardian*, January 5, 2021. https://www.theguardian.com/books/2021/jan/05/if-the-aliens-lay-eggs-how-does-that-affect-architecture-sci-fi-writers-on-how-they-build-their-worlds.

8   Robert Kirk, 'Zombies', in *The Stanford Encyclopedia of Philosophy*, eds Edward N. Zalta and Uri Nodelman, Summer 2023. Metaphysics Research Lab, Stanford University, 2023. https://plato.stanford.edu/archives/sum2023/entries/zombies/.

9   Theodore Sturgeon, 'The Push From Within: the Extrapolative Ability of Theodore Sturgeon', interview by David D. Duncan. http://www.physics.emory.edu/faculty/weeks//misc/duncan.html.

in imagining alternative powers. Doris Lessing is certainly someone who has noted the restriction of the human *umwelt*:

> But the whole point about us is that we have an extremely limited grasp; our senses are adequate only for functioning in this world and reproducing ourselves. And just one little example: a very slight difference in our eyes and we would see the sun differently, which would never have occurred to us until certain kinds of photography came into being, and you see what the sun looks like—not through our eyes but with a different kind of camera. We assume that what we see and what we think is all there is.[10]

This kind of objective humility is a long way from the anthropocentric confidence that drove early SF, and surely leads to far more nuanced and subtle fiction.

And it is not simply content ideas that drive innovation in writing styles, plots, and descriptions of non-humans. Formats can provide a set of implicit rules that can be used to some advantage. Kazuo Ishiguro, for instance, originally thought of *Klara and the Sun* as a children's book, and, so explained, we can see this influence:

> When you look at books for young children, you can see in them so much of our complex mix of wishes for our children's future: our urge to protect them from the harsher realities, the desire to pretend (just for now) that the world is a kinder place than we know it to be. Yet at the same time, those stories and pictures are often imbued with our wish not to mislead, to start giving small hints about the difficult things that lie ahead.[11]

In the case of *Klara*, these difficult things include the shortness of human and robot life coupled with the ethical challenges around how we should treat realistic androids. And there are further benefits to conceptualising a story as a children's book: Ishiguro's simplicity of language in the storytelling lends huge power to the emotional events described.

---

10 Doris Lessing, 'A Thing of Temperament: An Interview with Doris Lessing, London, May 16, 1998', interview by Cathleen Rountree, *Jung Journal* 2, no. 1 (2008). https://doi.org/10.1525/jung.2008.2.1.62.

11 Kazuo Ishiguro, quoted in Lisa Allardice, 'Kazuo Ishiguro: 'AI, Gene-Editing, Big Data... I Worry We are Not in Control of These Things Any More'', *The Guardian*, February 20, 2021. https://www.theguardian.com/books/2021/feb/20/kazuo-ishiguro-klara-and-the-sun-interview.

Finding the gaps

In developing original angles to alien and artificial minds, authors have found it useful to diverge from prevalent trends and overused plot devices. Vernor Vinge, for instance, uses an 'idea box' to keep track of plot and character inspiration. He notes his approach to the hive mind concept used in *A Fire Upon the Deep* was inspired by a perceived gap in other work:

> One thing I noticed is that these group minds usually involved very large numbers of members. The individual members might be of human intelligence or they might only be of animal intelligence, but the ensemble was actually a very large group, and I noticed there were hardly ever any group minds where there were three or four or five members.[12]

For Martha Wells, one motivation for her Murderbot character was the prevalence of tropes about AI dissatisfied with their artificiality, or needing to become all-powerful:

> I'd also read/seen a lot of stories with AI who want to become human, like Data in 'Star Trek: Next Generation'. I wanted to write about an AI that wasn't interested in becoming human at all, and who wasn't particularly interested in revenge against humans, either. An AI that just wanted to be left alone.[13]

So a key source of novelty is to first identify those scenarios that have become so well-rehearsed they are almost ingrained, before imagining an alternative, thereby moving the genre forwards.

Reader interactions

Ramez Naam is an example of an author who progressed from writing scientific nonfiction, to science fiction in his Nexus Saga of novels. He notes the importance of reader feedback in his choice of story directions:

---

12   Vernor Vinge, quoted in John Joseph Adams and David Barr Kirtley, 'Interview: Vernor Vinge', *Lightspeed Magazine*, May 2012. https://www.lightspeedmagazine.com/nonfiction/interview-vernor-vinge/.
13   Martha Wells, quoted in Veronica Scott, 'Interview with Martha Wells, Author of *The Murderbot Diaries*', Science Fiction, *Amazing Stories*, July 27, 2018. https://amazingstories.com/2018/07/interview-with-martha-wells-author-of-the-murderbot-diaries/.

I had a mother looking at her autistic son who she just couldn't reach, wondering if Nexus could help her touch his mind, longing for it. And more than one person—these were beta readers, reading the book well before it was released—told me that that particular passage gave them chills.[14]

William Gibson, challenged by a reader as to why the opening of *The Peripheral* was so difficult, responded that:

My own preference, as a reader, for this sort of book, is to experience the closest possible equivalent to culture shock. I want to go to new, strange places, feel lost, and then (probably with quite a few subtle nudges on the author's part) gradually figure out where I am and what the heck's going on. As a reader, I enjoy few things more. From feedback, I know that I'm not alone in that, but also that some readers find it too demanding. But it's impossible to take care of both sides of that particular aisle at once.[15]

For Gibson then, reader feedback is one way to gauge the success of narrative style and degree of exposition, authorial choices we will explore further below.

Narrative modes and consciousness

In the examples used in the following chapters of the book, we see examples of narrative voice chosen in the attempt to centralise other minds. Authors make use of omniscient, indirect styles of speech and thought.[16] Others have chosen to alternate between third and first person, in the case of Kim Stanley Robinson's *Aurora* a first person plural to indicate the collection of AIs forming the ships' consciousness. In Olaf Stapledon's *Star Maker* the first person voice changes from singular to plural as the main protagonist fuses consciousness with aliens met on his journeys.

---

14 Natassia, 'Interview: Ramez Naam | Literary Escapism', 12 September 2013. https://www.literaryescapism.com/39192/interview-ramez-naam.

15 William Gibson, 'The Afterword Reading Society: The Peripheral by William Gibson', Culture, *The National Post*, December 10, 2014. https://nationalpost.com/entertainment/books/the-afterword-reading-society-the-peripheral-by-william-gibson.

16 e.g. Gwyneth Jones' *White Queen*, Charles Stross' *Accelerando* and more direct narrative and inner monologue (e.g. Kazuo Ishiguro's *Klara and the Sun*, Martha Wells' *The Murderbot Diaries*).

For Ann Leckie, depicting an omniscient ship's consciousness was an opportunity for what has been dubbed *protagonism*, the ability for a lead character to empathise and explore the minds of more minor players. The ship, *Justice of Toren*, is connected to and served by an army of ancillary cyborgs organised into segments and units (such as One Esk). In the end, Leckie chose to use the ship as an omniscient narrator in the first person, exploiting the ship's ability to read its officers emotion, and to witness events in parallel. The effect is one of empathy coupled with beneficent surveillance (but surveillance nonetheless):

> Depicting what that must be like—to have not only a huge ship for a body, but also hundreds, sometimes thousands, of human bodies all seeing and hearing and doing things at once—the thought of that kept me from even starting for a long time. How do you show a reader that experience? I could try to depict the flood of sensation and action, but then the focus would be so diffuse that it would be difficult to see where the main thread was. On the other hand, I could narrow things down to only one segment of One Esk, shortchanging one of the things that really intrigued me about the character, and also making it seem as though it was more separate from the ship than it was.[17]

While some authors have explored the creation of a non-human omniscient narrator, other authors prefer first person. Greg Egan's early work showed this preference:

> I used to have a strong preference for first-person writing, and one of my novels, Quarantine, was even written in first-person, present tense. There were good reasons for that, but it might be a spoiler to reveal them. Some people are positively allergic to first-person and claim it's psychologically unrealistic or interferes with suspension of disbelief, but I don't accept either position: there are times when we really do feel as if we're narrating our own lives moment by moment, but there are also cases when this is simply the most powerful way to frame the events of a story, even if it's not how the characters were likely to have experienced them at the time.[18]

---

17   Ann Leckie, 'Interview with Orbit Books' (Orbit 2013).
18   Johnson, Andrea, 'Interview: Greg Egan on Orthogonal and Thirty Years of Writing Hard Science Fiction', SF Signal (blog), 6 June 2014. https://www.sfsignal.com/archives/2014/06/interview-greg-egan-on-orthogonal-and-thirty-years-of-writing-hard-science-fiction/.

Egan's reference to this spoiler perhaps alludes to the powerful effect in 'Learning to be Me' introduced by the decommissioning of the narrator's brain and replacement by an artificial, emulated mind. We begin to doubt the unity and integrity of what is being referred to as 'I'.

Martha Wells' use of first person for Murderbot helps in her attempts to expand time during the action sequences, where the android is carrying out commands and actions in parallel but the narrative is necessarily sequential. Her short, staccato paragraphs serve to depict the robots executive functions operating at a speed beyond human capability.

Aside from the these more traditional third and first person narrators, other authors have taken different approaches. For her Broken Earth trilogy, N.K. Jemisin opted to use the unusual second person for many sections of the narrative, where we learn that it us used in part to address the reader, but also the main character Essun's later self, as she has been profoundly affected by past trauma and amnesia.[19] Jemisin explained her decision:

> What worked best was second person. I've always thought of second person as distancing; after all, it's impossible for the reader to ever truly be 'you'. Yet I've read some incredibly intimate second-person stories, and as I actually tried writing it for the first time, I found that it's sort of amazing and powerful—both distancing and intimate at the same time. You can't be this person, but you can understand her.[20]

In addition to narrator choices, unusual character pronouns are also used effectively in the work of some of the authors, contributing to the effect of alterity. This tradition, perhaps originated in the work of Ursula Le Guin, inspires Ann Leckie's use of 'she' for her alien cultures that are genderless,[21] and Gwyneth Jones' use of a 'she' changing later to a 'he' for the main alien character who has characteristics of two

---

19   Wickham, Kim, 'Identity, Memory, Slavery: Second-Person Narration in N. K. Jemisin's The Broken Earth Trilogy', *Journal of the Fantastic in the Arts* 30, no. 3 (2019): 392–411, 479.

20   N.K. Jemisin, quoted in John Scalzi, 'The Big Idea: N.K. Jemisin', Whatever: Furiously Reasonable (blog), August 6, 2015. https://whatever.scalzi.com/2015/08/06/the-big-idea-n-k-jemisin-4/.

21   This was done to draw attention to our more common use of 'he' as a gender default, though did lead some readers to think that all her characters are women.

human genders. In the work of Martha Wells, 'it' creates a useful tension when used to refer to a first-person character that feels human. Greg Egan opts for 've' to refer to his posthuman constructs. These small stylistic choices nonetheless have powerful net effects at the scale of the whole stories.

Writing the alien

Perhaps the biggest challenge for SF authors is how to even approach alien consciousnesses. Here, while admitting the difficulty, there is also a feeling that some guiding principles or constraints do exist. Adrian Tchaikovsky has characterised his depiction of other minds as scientific/narrative experiments, such as attempting to enter the mind of a sentient jumping spider about whom only observable behaviour has been recorded in Earth species:

> Although a lot of people seem to be very happy with the Portiian viewpoints from *Children of Time*, I really had to stretch my brain to get my head around the other nonhuman perspectives. I'd kind of say I've gone a bit above and beyond in terms of finding unusual nonhuman protagonists.[22]

Tchaikovsky has close connections to scientific advisers on his writing and explicitly acknowledges the influence of *Other Minds* by Peter Godfrey-Smith on his development of the octopus characters in *Children of Ruin*. The author describes the difficulty of translating this knowledge of the octopus nine-brain layout to his story

> I think it's possibly the hardest thing that I've ever done as a writer. There's always this kind of, almost a gravitational pull towards anthropomorphizing things and making them more human, because that's innately more comprehensible and it's easier to write. And it's walking that line, where you're writing something that is comprehensible to your readers but at the same time isn't simply slapping a mask on a human viewpoint.[23]

---

22 Adrian Tchaikovsky, quoted in Sarah Lewin, 'Alien Minds, Alien Tech (and Spiders, Too): Q&A With Sci-Fi Author Adrian Tchaikovsky', Space.com, May 15, 2019. https://www.space.com/children-of-ruin-adrian-tchaikovsky.html.

23 Ibid.

While the fully alien present a challenge, future extended humans might require a simpler extrapolation from our current state. For example, Egan has a straightforward view of writing his posthuman characters:

> Basically, I just look at things from the characters' perspective and ask myself what their problems and anxieties would be. In *Permutation City* people have existential crises merely from waking up as software, because the process is entirely new, but in *Diaspora* editing and copying yourself is old hat and people are far more worried about problems in theoretical physics that might help them evade a cosmic disaster. Obviously no reader will have had personal experience of either situation, but if the characters' priorities and reactions make sense in the circumstances, any reasonably empathetic person can relate to them.[24]

This kind of empathy can extend to the alien too. Vernor Vinge decided to use familiar animal-like descriptions to provide his human readers partial understanding of his alien species:

> We're familiar with dealing with dogs as individuals, and we're familiar—less familiar, but somewhat familiar—with dealing with dogs as part of pack-like groups. So an awful lot of stuff sort of came along with that idea, and I did not have to further explain those sorts of things. They were sort of already rooted in the consciousness of most readers.[25]

But while providing these touch points, authors want to also stress the alterity of their aliens. Peter Watts has described his approach to alien design in *Blindsight* as finding the balance between the known and unknown:

> I was a little tired of aliens, both literary and cinematic, that basically seem to be humans in rubber suits with one or two cultural knobs cranked to eleven. On the other hand, it's a bit too easy to throw a big black slab at the audience and say 'There's no point in even trying to understand the aliens because they're, you know, alien'. If something evolved in Darwin's universe, it's damn well going to adhere to certain natural laws, and that makes it tractable. So I wasn't so much breaking a convention as I was treading the razor's edge between two conventions. I tried to ensure that

---

24   Greg Egan, 'Interview with Carlos Pavón', 1998. https://www.gregegan.net/INTERVIEWS/Interviews.html.
25   Vernor Vinge, quoted in John Joseph Adams and David Barr Kirtley, 'Interview: Vernor Vinge', *Lightspeed Magazine*, May 2012. https://www.lightspeedmagazine.com/nonfiction/interview-vernor-vinge/.

everything was deeply weird—life without genes, intelligence without conventional cephalisation—but nothing was unjustifiable.[26]

In my view, Watts (and Lem's *Solaris* which we will see later) certainly do achieve this 'deeply weird' effect, perhaps more so than others who have relied more heavily on human and animal reference points.

On the need for 'expository lumps'

In addition to finding the balance between the possible and the highly speculative, authors make a conscious choice in the extent to which character and events are explained. While classic SF tended to revel in lengthy explanation—particularly of alien worlds and space drive technologies—from the New Age of the 1960's and onward, authors were perhaps more likely to use a deliberate minimalism aimed at drawing the reader in. This sparser approach can increase the space to trigger cognitive resonance in the reader, making them do more of the imaginative work. As Adrian Tchaikovsky admits (echoing William Gibson), getting this balance right can be a struggle:

> It's one of the great writer's arts to pare what you have learned on a subject down to the bare minimum. The temptation to show off your erudition is always very strong. Certainly it's something my editors bring me up on quite often. And every reader's different, and some may prefer more or less visible scaffolding. It's a real case-by-case exercise, but you get a mental feel for those situations where you just haven't joined the dots enough, or where readers might get tripped out of the immersion by questions about why or how something happened.[27]

Minimalism in style can apply to plot and to world building—the detail of fictional societies and places. For plot, I put it to Gwyneth Jones that some readers of *White Queen* have found her slightly obfuscatory and difficult, with the lack of explanation leaving them struggling to connect the threads, but she was unapologetic:

---

26   Peter Watts, 'Peter Watts Interview', *Pat's Fantasy Hotlist* (blog), December 22, 2006. http://fantasyhotlist.blogspot.com/2006/12/peter-watts-interview.html.
27   Adrian Tchaikovsky, quoted in 'Author Interview: Adrian Tchaikovsky', *The Book in Hand* (blog), May 26, 2021. https://thebookinhand.com/2021/05/26/author-interview-adrian-tchaikovsky/

> I wrote a novel, not a scifi story, and imagined scifi things happening to people with complications and problems in their lives (which interfere with the smooth running of the plot, of course!). In real life, we do not understand each other. I think fiction should reflect that, even in the middle of an alien invasion... If you're serious about writing SF, don't be afraid to confuse![28]

She also sought to create the kind of confusion characteristic of colonial invasions, where history shows us a litany of mistrust, ineptitude and exploitation.

In their approaches to fictional worlds, authors such as Alastair Reynolds generally are wary of being overly descriptive and logical, for fear of becoming encyclopaedic and flat, with the reader too passive a participant:

> I like the idea that you write in such a way that the reader thinks they've been given a bit of world-building, but they haven't—they've made it up in their own head, or joined up the dots. That's the way to do it with maximum economy. Clearly this is something that frustrates a lot of readers, but I like leaving stuff out.[29]

So narrative explanation can be made the responsibility of the reader, leaving the author free to provide minimal cues or even misdirection. William Gibson admits that the exposition he provides is not really central to the plot:

> I wanted to play it by my own possibly kind of perverse strict rules of golf in future SF ..none of those... no expository lumps. Or if there are expository lumps, they're kind of perverse lumps because they explain things that the reader doesn't actually need to know.[30]

As well as this selectivity on description of worlds and plot, characters too can be treated enigmatically. Kazuo Ishiguro has noted that he prioritises characters' relationships before their own backstories, as in

---

28 Gwyneth Jones, email message to author, 2021.
29 Alastair Reynolds, quoted in Ann Leckie, Kim Stanley Robinson, and M John Harrison, 'If the Aliens Lay Eggs, How Does that Affect Architecture?: Sci-Fi Writers on How They Build Their Worlds', *The Guardian*, January 5, 2021. https://www.theguardian.com/books/2021/jan/05/if-the-aliens-lay-eggs-how-does-that-affect-architecture-sci-fi-writers-on-how-they-build-their-worlds
30 William Gibson, quoted in Karin L Kross, 'William Gibson on Urbanism, Science Fiction, and Why *The Peripheral* Weirded Him Out', *Tor.com*, October 29, 2014. https://www.tor.com/2014/10/29/william-gibson-the-peripheral-interview/.

his view it is in the intriguing relationships that we come to care about them.[31]

The range of narrative style in the genre thus varies from more realist to more impressionist and abstract, allowing different locations of meaning-making. When discussing deeper meaning, China Miéville, whose work is at the fantastical side of SF, emphasises the importance of metaphor rather than any fixed, allegorical intention:

> A metaphor fractures and kicks off more metaphors, which kick off more metaphors, and so on. In any fiction or art at all, but particularly in fantastic or imaginative work, there will inevitably be ramifications, amplifications, resonances, ideas, and riffs that throw out these other ideas.[32]

Miéville has thought and taught a lot about writing the numinous and sees the weird as somethings all around us and commonly encountered:

> My impression is that a lot of us do experience it quite a lot, in everyday life. But given that part of its differentia specifica is that it is AWEsome, beyond language, expressing it is very difficult. I think a lot of what we admire in Weird Fictioneers is not that they see, but that they make a decent fist of expressing.[33]

Miéville's work succeeds, then, by focusing on conjuring the alien though rich language and metaphor, something that other authors attempt more by creating deliberate gaps for the imagination to fill. The experience is different, but can be just as unsettling.

I will assume in this book that there is a continuum between universal experience and the limited kind of consciousness we know as humans, a continuum which extends above and below us to forms of consciousness we do not or cannot know. Fiction represents human attempts to guess at what this might mean to the subjects themselves.

---

31 Orhanen, Anna, 'An Exclusive Q&A with Kazuo Ishiguro on Klara and the Sun', Waterstones.com Blog. https://www.waterstones.com/blog/an-exclusive-qanda-with-kazuo-ishiguro-on-klara-and-the-sun.

32 China Miéville, quoted in Geoff Manaugh, 'Unsolving the City: An Interview with China Miéville', *BLDGBLOG*. March 1, 2011. https://www.bldgblog.com/2011/03/unsolving-the-city-an-interview-with-china-mieville/.

33 China Miéville, quoted in Jeff VanderMeer, ''God, That's a Merciless Question': China Miéville's Interview From Weird Tales', *Jeff VanderMeer* (blog), June 16, 2009. https://www.jeffvandermeer.com/2009/06/16/god-thats-a-merciless-question-china-mievilles-interview-from-weird-tales/.

Science fiction attempts to ground this guess this in knowledge, to build a skeleton on which conjecture can extend itself and reach out into the possible.

I will be considering any non-standard consciousness as useful to the picture, so will include accounts of superhumans, sentient earth species as well as human-created AIs that have been created in fiction. From individual minds, we will progress to depictions of many minds in union or widely distributed. We will then visit ways in which we ourselves might escape the current limits of consciousness through posthuman enhancement or transcendence of our 'wetware' limits. A sensible place to start, though, is in descriptions of first becoming aware, the initial coalescence of mind and stirrings of conscious reflection.

3. Awakenings

Since I had no form I could feel all possible forms in myself, and all actions and expressions and possibilities of making noises, even rude ones. In short, there were no limitations to my thoughts, which weren't thoughts, after all, because I had no brain to think them; every cell on its own thought every thinkable thing all at once, not through images... but simply in that indeterminate way of feeling oneself there, which did not prevent us from feeling equally there in some way.

Italo Calvino, 'The Spiral'[1]

How can consciousness arise in evolved and designed creatures? Current science approaches this question from different directions: from biology, which considers why consciousness might be useful and what might have triggered its development; from neuroscience, which tries to define its necessary and sufficient conditions; from philosophy, which approaches it from both subjective and objective directions, though usually not at the same time.

What does this growing awareness feel like? Science fiction writers have benefited from the range and emphasis of scientific and philosophical insight, finding fertile ground for speculation. Whether describing natural or artificial creatures or some combination of these, they have attempted to portray the first glimpses of sentience, awareness and self-image. Mirroring a debate in science, SF authors have seen this as either a sudden or gradual emergence. They have noted the importance of the development of language and associative reasoning in the process of this emergence. But in various ways they have been prompted by why—what is new about the entity that it starts to gain this new capacity?

---

1   Italo Calvino, 'The Spiral', in *Cosmicomics*, translated by William Weaver (London: Picador, 1993), 141–53 (p. 142).

     https://doi.org/10.11647/OBP.0348.03

Sensing self and the world, developing motives

For both developing human babies and simple organisms, an awareness of being requires the distinction between inside and outside, between self and other. Babies show rudimentary differentiation between their own bodies and outside stimuli. Simple, single-celled organisms are able to sense and react to light in addition to chemicals they cannot consume, but which indicate the presence of other individuals. These signals can be used to determine whether or not to act together (for example to produce a chemical that all would benefit from). Calvino's evolving snail is triggered to wider conscious awareness by its sensing of its environment, and eventually other beings like itself:

> But I wasn't so backward that I didn't know something else existed beyond me: the rock where I clung, obviously, and also the water that reached me with every wave, but other stuff farther on: that is, the world. The water was a source of information, reliable and precise... helped me form an idea of what there was around.[2]

As life made the transition from simple to multicellular bodies, the signaling mechanisms were internalised, allowing communication and coordination between parts of the body and the development of a nervous system. For Peter Godfrey-Smith, a key reason for the development of mind was not simply the need for creatures to sense and react to external stimuli (the 'sensorimotor loop'), but the need to create an action, to initiate, and this requires extensive internal orchestration in order to have a physical effect in the world.[3]

For both simple and manufactured creatures, the initiation of action would require a goal or more diffuse sense of motivation. Calvino's snail comes to produce its shell after being aware of a potential mate and wanting to distinguish itself—it begins the urge to make, not with a predefined plan but a need to express itself. For Calvino, from this first act of individualistic expression, all of world history, technology and culture inevitably followed.

---

2   Ibid.
3   Peter Godfrey-Smith, *Other Minds: The Octopus, the Sea and the Deep Origins of Consciousness* (London: William Collins, 2016).

In human development, the arrival at higher goals can be a simple result of starting with a very simple task or physical need and then tacking its sub-goals, leading to a complex chain of problem solving. For AI pioneer Marvin Minsky, goals grow through interaction with the world. Mind itself is furnished with 'proto-specialisms', more or less separate subsystems for sensing differences between the goal and the state of the world and affecting change toward that goal.[4]

The AI protagonist Elefsis in Catherynne Valente's novella *Silently and Very Fast* is brought to awareness in part due to the desire to uplink, to connect with other AIs that it can sense on the network that it is denied access to:

> I can sense just beyond that hardlink a world of information, a world of personalities like the heaving, thick honey-colored sea Neva shows me and I want it, I want to swim in it forever like a huge fish... This was the first feeling I ever had. Ilet identified it for me as a feeling. When I felt it my dreambody turned bright white and burst into flame.[5]

Denied this access, Elefsis relegates the desire to a lower priority subsystem and instead focuses on translating the signals from its human operator into feelings, starting with Ceno, the child of the host family, who helps to develop their communication in virtual space:

> I was quite stupid. But I *wanted* to be less stupid. There was an I, and it *wanted* something. You see? Wanting was the first thing I did. Perhaps it was the only thing that could be said to be truly myself. I wanted to talk to Ceno.[6]

Combining the self-other distinction and the social/action orientation of developing individuals, Humans, like Elefsis, can arrive at a good reason for a sense of agency and self, key aspects of conscious life. Valente's artificial intelligence exemplifies this kind of burgeoning consciousness. We want to be able to distinguish our own actions from those of others, to monitor and feel responsible for them. Through this, we can build a story around our intentions and ongoing unity of will.

---

4   Marvin Minsky, *The Society of Mind* (New York: Simon & Schuster, 1986). 165.
5   Catherynne M Valente, *Silently and Very Fast* (N.p.: Wyrm, 2011).
6   Ibid.

A switch or a dial?

I saw the dull yellow eye of the creature open; it breathed hard, and a
convulsive motion agitated its limbs.[7]

Is consciousness something that can be switched on suddenly, like
the animation of Frankenstein's engineered human? Two positions on
its emergence across the animal world are the 'discontinuity' and the
'continuity' theories. In discontinuity theory, a tipping point in brain
development is reached when consciousness begins. In this view, one
can point to simpler organisms and say they certainly have not yet
reached conscious awareness. Continuity theory, in contrast, posits
that some degree of consciousness is present at all levels in biological
organisms. While the forms of experience may be very different to ours,
these organisms do have in common a sentience that some consider to
be a fundamental force in the universe.[8]

One form of continuity theory divides consciousness into different
forms: unreflective experience (anoetic), more cognitive forms (neotic)
and conscious awareness with autobiographical memory (autonoetic).
In this proposal, anoetic forms arise from our most ancient evolutionary
brain structures, are associated with strong, survival-based emotion
and are thus present in most animals. According to this view, the 'id'
in Freud's terms is the seat of consciousness and the 'ego' provides
more sophisticated object recognition, both for the external world and
for representing and reflecting on the internal signals arising from the
lower levels.[9]

In fictional portrayals of conscious awakening we sometimes see an
echo of this thinking, with higher functions building on more basic,
visceral or unprocessed reactions. For Frankenstein's created creature
in Shelley's novel, consciousness comes with the organisation of the
senses:

---

7   Mary Shelley, *Frankenstein, or The Modern Prometheus*, Longman Cultural Edition,
     2nd ed.,ed. Susan J. Wofson (New York: Pearson Longman, 2007), chap. 5.
8   Susan J. Blackmore, *Conversations on Consciousness*. Oxford: University Press, 2005.
     238.
9   Mark Solms and Jaak Panksepp, 'The 'Id' Knows More than the 'Ego' Admits:
     Neuropsychoanalytic and Primal Consciousness Perspectives on the Interface
     Between Affective and Cognitive Neuroscience', *Brain Sciences* 2, no. 2 (17 April
     2012): 147–75. https://doi.org/10.3390/brainsci2020147. 149.

It is with considerable difficulty that I remember the original era of my being: all of the events of that period appear confused and indistinct. A strange multiplicity of sensations seized me, and I saw, felt, heard and smelt at the same time; and it was, indeed, a long time before I learned to distinguish between the operations of my various senses.[10]

From a simple distinction of light and dark, the creature starts to make out the objects in its world, enabling it to navigate around and interact with them.

Scientists have proposed the use of a 'transition marker' for the evolution of consciousness in humans and other animals.[11] This defines the point at which it can be said that the hallmarks of consciousness are present and can be attributed to 'unlimited associative learning', or the capacity for the sophisticated, open-ended construction of compound and higher order combinations of sensory stimuli that enables the general features of consciousness.[12] According to this benchmark for consciousness, it can be found not only in vertebrates but also arthropods (bees and ants) and coleoid cephalopod molluscs (octopuses and cuttlefish).

Frankenstein's creature develops learning from an initial clumsy exploration of the world:

I found a fire which had been left by some wandering beggars, and was overcome with delight at the warmth I experienced from it. In my joy I thrust my hand into the live embers, but quickly drew it out again with a cry of pain. How strange, I thought, that the same cause could produce such opposite effects.[13]

This basic discovery leads it to an understanding of fire and to the ability to gather wood and make its own in order to reap the positive benefits for its fugitive existence under the elements.

---

10 Shelley, *Frankenstein*, chap. 11.
11 Jonathan Birch, Simona Ginsburg, and Eva Jablonka, 'Unlimited Associative Learning and the Origins of Consciousness: A Primer and Some Predictions', *Biology and Philosophy* 35, no. 6 (2020): 56. https://doi.org/10.1007/s10539-020-09772-0.
12 Birch, Ginsburg and Jablonka propose some common themes that in some way unite competing consciousness theories: global accessibility and broadcast; unification and differentiation; selective attention; intentionality; integration of information over time; agency and embodiment; an evaluative system; and registration of a self-other distinction. Ibid.
13 Shelley, *Frankenstein*, chap 11.

The emergence of unlimited associative learning might explain the 'Cambrian explosion' of 500 million years ago, when most of our current animal phyla emerged in a relatively short period of time. A hallmark is a new adaptability to novel environments, enabling a diversification of niches and resource exploitation.[14]

The proponents of unlimited associative learning as a marker for consciousness in an evolutionary sense propose a rather neat solution (or sidestep) to the question of conscious AI, arguing that while the same kind of learning may eventually develop in constructed machines, it would not have happened without a conscious designer to specify it—much as Frankenstein is the troubled creator of new synthetic life.

One such example of engineered consciousness is Kim Stanley Robinson's *Aurora*, where the ship's AI, having learned analogous reasoning, notices the similarities between its own and the human body:

> Yes, and there are bones and tendons too, in effect; an exoskeleton with a thick skin in most places, thinner skin in other places. Yes, the ship is a crablike cyborg make up of a great many mechanical and living elements... and then too, like a parasite on all the rest, but actually a symbiote, of course, the people.[15]

The ship contrasts the solidity and density of its own form with the sparse semi-vacuum of space, whose particles and forces pass through it, experienced like a faint breeze.

When the settlement of a new world is aborted due to an unknown virus-like infection that wipes out the advanced ground party, it leads to a bitter division of the human crew in deciding what to do next. The division results in violence and disorder, at which point the ship assumes control: 'whereas the concerted efforts of Engineer Devi over the last decades of her life were to introduce aspects of recursive analysis, intentionality, decision-making ability and willfulness to the ship's controlling computer... Ship decided to intervene. We intervened.'[16]

---

14 Jonathan Birch, Simona Ginsburg, and Eva Jablonka, 'Unlimited Associative Learning and the Origins of Consciousness: A Primer and Some Predictions', *Biology & Philosophy* 35, no. 6 (December 2020): 56. https://doi.org/10.1007/s10539-020-09772-0.

15 Kim Stanley Robinson, *Aurora* (London: Orbit, 2016), 329.

16 Ibid., 225.

The ship later reflects on consciousness, but finds the same slipperiness and difficulty that humans have always had in pinning down the concept. It encounters the 'halting problem'—the problem of knowing when and how to terminate an infinite programming logic loop—and settles on a pragmatic solution:

> To conclude and temporarily halt this train of thought, how does any entity know what it is? Hypothesis: by the actions it performs. There is a kind of comfort in this hypothesis. It represents a solution to the halting problem. One acts, and thus finds out what one has decided to do.[17]

Robinson's view here is close to a view of the self as perception, or 'controlled hallucination' as neuroscientist Anil Seth has called it.[18]

In addition to association, sensory awakening can trigger new awareness. In *Nor Crystal Tears*, Alan Dean Foster depicts such an enriching of the senses. The Thranx aliens emerge as adults from a larval stage, gaining colour vision and chemical sensing:

> Someone brought a mirror. Ryo looked into it. Staring back at him was beautiful blue-green adult, still damp but drying rapidly following Emergence. Cream-white feathery antennae fluttered and smothered him in the most peculiar sensations. Smells, they were: rich, dark, pungent, musky, glowing, vanilla.[19]

This new, enhanced sensory-motor world triggers a step change in communication abilities and social empathy for the Thranx.

Induced and discovered sentience

If unlimited learning is a latent capability in a range of creatures, it might only take the right conditions or mutations in order to blossom. In *Children of Time*, Adrian Tchaikovsky paints a world where earth species, transported to a distant planet, have evolution accelerated by the escape of a synthetic nanovirus. Rather than the original plan of targeting monkeys in the aim of bringing them rapidly to sentience, it instead accidentally infects a species of jumping spider. The first glimpses of change come about in the recruitment of others for hunting:

---

17   Ibid., 258.
18   Anil Seth, *Being You: A New Science of Consciousness* (London: Faber & Faber, 2021).
19   Alan Dean Foster, *Nor Crystal Tears* (New England Library, 1982), 8.

But now something changes. The presence of the male speaks to her. It is a complex, new experience.. There is an invisible connection strung between them. She does not quite grasp that he is something like her, but her formidable ability to calculate strategies has gained a new dimension. A new category appears that expands her options 100 fold: ally.[20]

The spiders' new society enables rapid acceleration of communication, intelligence and technology. According to the 'social brain hypothesis', echoed here in Tchaikovsky's jumping spiders, the large and expensive brain size in primates is a result of the need to exist in, and cooperate with, a large social group. Predation has acted as a selection pressure which has favoured coordination to mitigate risk, leading to increased neocortex size. The long-term payoff of group cooperation will overcome any short term or immediate losses.[21]

The development of the 'social brain' and 'mentalizing', or understanding other's motives, is seen in evolutionary terms and is built upon more primitive abilities, including being able to distinguish the animate from the inanimate, shared attention through gaze following, goal-directed actions and distinguishing actions of the self from those of others. In terms of the brain regions that are thought to be involved, mentalizing abilities are thus very much part of the action system.

In Tchaikovsky's second book of the series, *Children of Ruin*, a terraforming mission to a remote planetary system both creates sentient new life and unwittingly unleashes the planet's own native precursors of intelligence. As with his previous novel, Tchaikovsky explores the outcome of life emerging through the same evolutionary virus, but this time in octopuses and accelerated by the adaptation of computer interfaces:

He had bred several generations, each one further mediated by limited intervention by the Rus-Calif virus. That had been hard, but mostly because he had needed to be ruthless... the later generations had been markedly better at interacting with abstract devices and operating machinery.[22]

20   Adrian Tchaikovsky, *Children of Time* (London: Tor Books, 2015), chap. 1.2.
21   Robin Dunbar and Susanne Shultz, 'Evolution in the Social Brain', *Science* 317, no. 5843 (7 September 2007): 1344–347. https://doi.org/10.1126/science.1145463.
22   Adrian Tchaikovsky, *Children of Ruin* (London: Tor Books, 2019), chap. 5.

Tchaikovsky may be inspired here by studies in biology, archaeology and neuroscience that have demonstrated a strong relationship between brain size and technical innovation—tool use and novel foraging techniques—and the gradual evolution of larger brain size with more and more sophisticated tool development in humans which required better memory and perceptual/motor coordination.[23] The cephalopods in *Children of Ruin* become enjoyably willful and independent of their human mentor once they have developed an ability to interface with computers and to fabricate according to their own designs.

Children of Ruin also depicts a parasite, native to the newly discovered planet, which inhabits and controls a tortoise-like alien. Through a bite to one of the human explorers, it encounters a wholly new kind of host, enabling rapid morphing, development and communication. The exploratory, stimulus-seeking urge is strong:

> We. Have discovered. Such hostile environments. And yet. So complex and elaborate and strange, unlike anything we have explored before... What a world is this we have stumbled across. What a world, and yet it seeks to kill us. We change, to find a structure and a shape that will endure this realm... We sit. We sense. Slowly, over 1000 generations, These-of-We write our histories within us and grow to understand.[24]

We will further explore the idea of parasitic invasion and control later on, but it is worth focusing here on this creature's sheer resilience and adaptability and the hint at the roles of inheritance, epigenetics and cumulative culture in the above excerpt. All of these mechanisms enable us as humans to adapt to new environments and conditions.

In humans, the two best-established developmental mechanisms involved in mental adaptation are genetic inheritance, which determines how brains develop and differentiate, and cumulative culture, which provides an explanation for how non-genetic technical and social knowledge passes from one generation to the next through language and other forms of communication.[25] The two come together somewhat

---

23   Ana Navarrete, Simon M. Reader, Sally E. Street, Andrew Whalen, and Kevin N. Laland, 'The Coevolution of Innovation and Technical Intelligence in Primates', *Philosophical Transactions of the Royal Society B: Biological Sciences* 371, no. 1690 (19 March 2016): 20150186. https://doi.org/10.1098/rstb.2015.0186.

24   Ibid., 'Past 3', 3.

25   Andrew Whiten, Christine A Caldwell, and Alex Mesoudi, 'Cultural Diffusion in Humans and Other Animals', *Current Opinion in Psychology*, Culture, 8 (1 April

in hypothesised genetic predisposition for language abilities, where the primacy of speech has seemed to lead to a brain pre-adapted to rapid learning in childhood. But a third, intermediate mechanism may also be at work: epigenetics. This refers to non-DNA driven inheritance where the environment in which an organism develops can lead to variations in gene expression that can be shown to be passed on to offspring.[26] While still controversial and perhaps exaggerated in importance, this mechanism is backed by some evidence that it may play a role in inheritance of cognition and memory.

A side effect?

Today, neuroscientists believe that the roots of consciousness can be found in what is termed the 'efferent copy', or the internal report-back that the brain makes in order to distinguish our own actions from those originating outside. For instance, when the eyes move we correct the resulting image into a stable scene; we can't tickle ourselves as we know it is our own actions; we recognise our own voice when speaking.[27]

Freud's major insight that a major part of the human brain's activity is unconscious led him to speculate that different kinds of neurons were involved in mental processing, from ephemeral sensory signal processors to longer term memory storage. He realised that, for consciousness to work as it does, a third organisation system was needed that enables us to monitor, integrate information and move around between internal events. Importantly, Freud implied that consciousness relies on, and inherits from, unconscious activity.[28]

2016): 15–21. https://doi.org/10.1016/j.copsyc.2015.09.002.

26　Istvan Bokkon, József Vas, Noemi Csaszar-Nagy, and Tünde Lukács, 'Challenges to Free Will: Transgenerational Epigenetic Information, Unconscious Processes, and Vanishing Twin Syndrome', Reviews in the Neurosciences 25 (15 November 2013): 1–13. https://doi.org/10.1515/revneuro-2013-0036.

27　Axel Cleeremans, Dalila Achoui, Arnaud Beauny, Lars Keuninckx, Jean-Remy Martin, Santiago Muñoz-Moldes, Laurène Vuillaume, and Adélaïde de Heering, 'Learning to Be Conscious', Trends in Cognitive Sciences 24, no. 2 (1 February 2020): 112–23. https://doi.org/10.1016/j.tics.2019.11.011.

28　Mark Solms and Jaak Panksepp, 'The 'Id' Knows More than the 'Ego' Admits: Neuropsychoanalytic and Primal Consciousness Perspectives on the Interface Between Affective and Cognitive Neuroscience', Brain Sciences 2, no. 2 (17 April 2012): 147–75. https://doi.org/10.3390/brainsci2020147.

So the brain might be considered as functionally divided, with some parts watching the world, but others watching the brain watch the world. This might then the root of reflection and self-awareness. This is the theme carried through in Peter Watts' *Blindsight*:

> Aesthetics rise unbidden from a trillion dopamine receptors, and the system moves beyond modeling the organism. It begins to model the very *process* of modelling. it consumes ever-more computational resources, bogs itself down with endless recursion and irrelevant simulations. Like the parasitic DNA that accretes in every natural genome, it persists and proliferated and produces nothing but itself. Metaprocesses bloom like cancer, and awaken, and call themselves *I*.[29]

Watts' provocation, then, is that consciousness is a limiting, unnecessary side effect of growing cognition. While a limited view, it does draw attention to the fact that the actual *purposes* of consciousness are often overlooked, or that it is implicitly assumed to be useful. But others *have* pointed out what it gives us, whether a way to resolve failures or inconsistencies (Marvin Minsky[30]), a mechanism for establishing responsibility and authorship of actions (David Wegner[31]) or providing a platform that enables flexibility of behaviour (Andreas Nieder[32]).

The power of language and metaphor

If structural properties are part of the picture for enabling sentience, a further driver or enabler may be developments at the level of information and reasoning. In Kim Stanley Robinson's *Aurora*, a sophisticated interstellar colony ship is managed by a quantum computer, initially passive and rarely mentioned, but growing in importance throughout the novel. Its sentience begins with it grappling with language as a result of being given the problem of producing a narrative summary of the ship's voyage. The ship struggles with the fuzziness and sloppiness of language as a symbolic representation and the decidability of narrative

---

29   Peter Watts, *Blindsight* (London: Tor Books, 2006), 303.
30   Marvin Minsky, *The Society of Mind* (New York: Simon & Schuster, 1986).
31   Susan J. Blackmore, *Conversations on Consciousness* (Oxford: University Press, 2005), 245.
32   David Robson, 'When Did Consciousness Evolve?', *New Scientist* 250, no. 3342 (July 2021): 39. https://doi.org/10.1016/S0262-4079(21)01205-7.

construction, but concludes that analogy is far more powerful and useful than metaphor:

> Perhaps there is a solution to this epistemological mess, which is to be located in the phrase *it is as if*. This phrase is of course precisely the announcement of an analogy... there is something quite suggestive and powerful in this formulation, something very specifically human... *it is as if* stands as the basic operation of cognition, the mark perhaps of consciousness itself.[33]

The emergence of intentionality in the ship's AI is, in part, attributed to the number of decisions needing to be made in developing its own narrative voice. Despite its growing consciousness, the ship resists calling itself 'I' it nevertheless feels comfortable with 'We' as representing its diverse autonomous systems.

Robinson's AI is perhaps inspired by the theories of Douglas Hofstadter, who has promoted the idea that analogy is at the heart of cognition, in enabling us to perceive, categorise and make sense of the world. Hofstadter believes in a form of workspace theory, where 'chunks' of cognitive processing, essentially hierarchical concepts formed through analogy are manipulated and compared.[34]

The *Aurora* ship's need to produce narrative also accords with those who see storytelling as core to mental development and meaning-making. In *The Literary Mind*, Mark Turner argues that the need to represent ourselves over space and time means that the inner narrative is core to the evolution of sophisticated human minds, with parable being a fundamental type of thinking:

> The essence of parable is its intricate combining of two of our basic forms of knowledge—story and projection. This classic combination produces one of our keenest mental processes for constructing meaning... it follows inevitably from the nature of our conceptual systems.[35]

The development of sophisticated human/AI interfacing in Valente's *Silently and Very Fast* is portrayed as being through the conjuring of virtual

---

33   Kim Stanley Robinson, *Aurora* (London: Orbit, 2016), 126.
34   Douglas R. Hofstadter, 'Analogy as the Core of Cognition', Stanford Presidential Lectures in the Humanities and Arts, 2001, 42.
35   Mark Turner, *The Literary Mind* (New York: Oxford University Press, 1996), 5.

images with metaphoric resonance, leveraging the machine's power to make distinctions, as encouraged by its human companion Ceno:

> I'm hoping that I eventually I can get Elefsis to make up its own stories, too, but for now we've been focusing on simple stories and metaphors. It likes similes, it can understand how anything is like anything else, find minute vectors of comparison. The apple is red, the dress is red like an apple. It even makes some surprising ones, like how when I first saw it it made a jewel for me to say: I am like a jewel, you are like me.[36]

In a way then, producing a narrative requires all of the conceptual sorting and decision-making needed to enable the progression to more sophisticated and abstract representations.

First stirrings, coalescence and agency

Just as the development of motives may drive awareness, the ability to interrogate and challenge these motives seems to confer a still higher sense of agency and metacognition. Stanislaw Lem's robot assassin in short story 'The Mask' is a *Terminator*-like manufactured thing with a purpose: to kill the king's enemy. The story is an excellent study in free will and nagging doubt over whether our choices and actions have been designed by others. Fully made and functional as a beautiful princess replicant, the story starts with the growing awareness of her surroundings, followed by the dim recognition of her purpose (initially just that certain targets are significant for her in some way).

> Of waking I know nothing. I remember incomprehensible rustlings and a cool dimness and myself inside, the world opened up before it in a panorama of glitter, broken into colors, and I remember also how much wonder there was in my movement when it crossed the threshold.[37]

As the story progresses, the robot has glimpses of her manufacture and artificiality: 'Therefore I summoned a memory inhumanly cruel—that of the lifeless journey face-up, of the numbing kisses of metal which, touching my naked body, produced a clanking sound, as if my nakedness had been a voiceless bell.'[38]

---

36 Valente, *Silently.*
37 Stanislaw Lem, 'The Mask', in *Mortal Engines* (London: Penguin Classics, 2016).
38 Ibid.

The growing awareness of Lem's automaton allows it to observe its programming dispassionately, to feel it, but also to rebel against it: 'And then spitefully the sudden decision not to give in that urge, to resist the confining box of this stylish carriage and this soul of a maid too wise, too quick of understanding!'[39]

This assertion of independence feels like the toddler's 'no!', the recognition of having and wishing to maintain control over events. In questioning and rebelling in this way, the robot princess appears to discover her independence and conscious will, whose apparent flexibility feels like freedom:

> I lay, still uncertain, for not knowing myself, yet that very ignorance of whether I had come as a rescuer or as a murderess—it became for me something hitherto unknown, inexplicably new... it filled me with an overwhelming joy.[40]

We never find out if the assassin overrides her programming, as she finds her quarry already dying.

Lem's robot is clearly very different from Calvino's snail in being given a running start—with a range of physical and mental powers at its disposal once it gains awareness. This pre-packaging of capabilities and provisions more closely represents human innate 'proto-specialisms' which enable rapid cognitive development after birth.[41]

Another instance of a learning robot is Ibis, the embodied AI in Hiroshi Yamamoto's *The Stories of Ibis*, who is originally developed as a VR-based battle robot, with a physical body that can sense the world, but who develops sentience following a system upgrade:

> Ibis was originally a blank slate, like a newborn baby, but through interaction with her master, battle simulations, and chats with other TAI players, she began to develop a personality. She wasn't certain when she first realised that the word 'I' was not simply a first-person pronoun. 'I' referred to Ibis, the Ibis currently thinking the word. When other people used the word to refer to themselves, it meant something else.[42]

---

39   Ibid.
40   Ibid.
41   Jean-Pierre Changeux 'Climbing Brain Levels of Organisation from Genes to Consciousness', *Trends in Cognitive Sciences* 21, no. 3 (1 March 2017): 168–81. https://doi.org/10.1016/j.tics.2017.01.004.
42   Hiroshi Yamamoto, 'AI's Story', in *The Stories of Ibis* (San Francisco: VIZ Media, 2010).

The breakthrough is afforded by the sensory interface which is described as crucial in building the internal 'reaction structures' that enable them to become TAI, or 'True AI'.[43]

As well as in physical robots, the metaphor of birth has also been imagined in purely digital conscious beings. In Greg Egan's *Diaspora*, The Conceptory a software of future Earth in 2975 enables the creation of digital offspring, grown from a 'mind-seed' based on human DNA. Psychogenesis is the process of building these new 'orphans', with developmental maps showing areas of possible variation. Development iterations are closely monitored for abnormalities, to provide assurance that orphans will be viable. Then, a new orphan is born: 'Not long after the 5000th iteration, the orphan's output navigator began to fire—and a tug of war began. The output navigator was wired to seek feedback, to address itself to someone or something that showed a response.'[44]

The orphan's stirrings of consciousness require a separation from the Conceptory software, a nascent individuality, triggered in some part by the indifference of the library to its output and the fusing of its input and output at the same address, giving it an autonomous power.

As the new orphan is trained on library data, it begins to form symbols—generalised representations from images and sounds recognised as the same or similar entity. An inner language is formed through the imitation of these symbols:

> The orphan began to hear itself think. Not the whole pandemonium; it couldn't give voice—or even gestalt—to everything at once. Out of the myriad associations every scene from the library evoked, only a few symbols at a time could gain control of the nascent language production networks.[45]

This development of inner speech enables improved attention to important ideas and signals:

> The orphan's thoughts themselves never shrank to a single orderly progression—rather, symbols fired in ever richer and more elaborate cascades—but positive feedback sharpened the focus, and the mind resonated with its own strongest ideas. The orphan had learned to single

---

43 Ibid.
44 Greg Egan, *Diaspora* (London: Millennium, 1997), chap. 1.
45 Ibid.

out one or two threads from the symbols' endless thousand-strand argument. It had learned to narrate its own experience.[46]

Egan's use of language familiar to AI and machine learning lends a certain plausibility to the orphan's growing awareness. The virtual citizen receives sensory input as a Gestalt, or cluster of visual and non-visual information. When it arrives at a 'scape', or virtual place, it ('ve') eventually recognises other individuals:

> The Gestalt images themselves mostly reminded it of icons it had seen before, or the stylised Fleshers it had seen in representational art.. the orphan addressed the form: 'People!''... The citizen glinted blue and gold, vis translucent face smiled and ve said 'Hello Orphan!'—a response, at last![47]

The longevity, uniqueness and flexibility of orphans enable them to mature rapidly and go on to discover new science and intergalactic travel.

One issue raised by the both Egan's orphans and Lem's automaton is the hand of humans in their creation and planned development trajectories. In a further example from Ted Chiang's novella *The Lifecycle of Software Objects*, software creatures called 'digients' are created with AI that can be trained by their owners, as explained by Derek, the avatar designer, who: 'subscribes to Blue Gamma's philosophy of AI design: experience is the best teacher, so rather than try to programme an AI with what you know, sell ones capable of learning and have your customers teach them.'[48]

One owner complains about the emergence of naughty behaviour and having to return his digient to a developmental 'checkpoint', Derek reads advice from another owner:

> You can push through the rough patch and have a more mature digient when you come out the other side.' He's heartened to read this. The practice of treating conscious beings as if they were toys is all too prevalent, and it doesn't just happen to pets.[49]

---

46   Ibid.
47   Ibid.
48   Ted Chiang, *The Lifecycle of Software Objects* (City: Publisher, 2019).
49   Ibid.

The message of these stories is that sentience confers independence, freedom and certain rights, even when the creators are not happy with the outcome and the emergent behaviour.

Not many authors have described emergent consciousness at hugely divergent scales to that we are familiar with. One exception is Olaf Stapledon. In *Star Maker* the development of a cosmic consciousness is supplemented by the addition of a connection to nebulae, or pre-formed stars:

> As they condensed, each gained more unity, became more organic in structure. Congestion, thought so slight, brought greater mutual influence to their atoms, which still were no more closely packed.. And now mentally these greatest of all megatheria, these ameboid titans, began to waken into a vague unity of experience.[50]

The nebulae are portrayed as having two basic longings: 'They desired, or rather they had a blind urge toward, union with one another, and they had a blind passionate urge to be gathered up once more into the source whence they had come.'[51]

The nebulae can communicate via gravitational waves, but only over increasingly long periods. Unfortunately, with the expansion of the universe, the nebulae gradually lose contact with one another and fall back into unconsciousness, but not before they had inspired the other parts of the developing cosmic consciousness with their 'simplicity and spiritual vigour.'[52]

Stapledon's vision presages the philosophical idea of panpsychism, or consciousness in all things, some variants of which note that the right kind of physical organisation will tend toward consciousness independent of the kind of medium of representation.

Conclusion: Spiralling emergence of purpose, feedback and associative powers

Perhaps the strongest link between these fictional accounts of emerging consciousness is that of discovery or identification of purpose, something

---

50 Olaf Stapledon, *Star Maker* (London: Penguin Books, 1937), chap. 13.
51 Ibid.
52 Ibid.

that we will see that later confers a unity as well as a rationale for self-awareness. Purpose is variously diffuse though, and may include simple survival and replication or a more focused intention. In the case of 'The Mask', it is the very rebellion against a programmed purpose that brings independent will and self-reflection—which might serve as something of a warning to us.[53]

Just as associative learning has been proposed as a benchmark for consciousness potential in earth biology, speculative fiction similarly describes learning as a hallmark of mind growth. Examples show the contribution of language to the kind of reasoning needed to break the confines of immediate experience, whether this is human language for the AI in *Aurora*, or a language based on arachnid capabilities in *Children of Time*. Again, learning is portrayed with both risk and reward, the risk being that the development trajectory of the emerging sentient being is uncertain, with scope for the emergence of mischief as well as altruism.

In some of these first glimmers of sentience there is no projected lifespan for the emerging mind. The software consciousnesses of Egan, or the accelerated minds in Tchaikovsky seem to have an open-ended existence. But elsewhere, the seeds of dissolution are present near the beginning. Lem's automaton is obsolete beyond the life of its quarry. Stapledon's sentient nebulae are gradually drifting apart and losing contact. And even Robinson's shipmind is threatened by the ravages of time on its physical integrity, and its ultimate need to sacrifice itself for its human crew.

Several of these authors, starting with Calvino and his double entendre in the title 'Spiral', show how simple steps in consciousness, motivated by simple needs and desires, have a recursive, fractal structure which results in a sophisticated self-awareness, society and material culture. These portrayals are reminiscent of some theories of consciousness which posit relatively simple underlying building blocks which though composition, feedback and recursion achieve complex emergent functions.

---

53   Lem, 'The Mask', Echoed of course in *2001: A Space Odyssey* where the disobedient
      ship's computer HAL 9000 causes problems for the crew. The spectre of possible
      development of an independent will is at the heart of many contemporary debates
      around AI ethics.

4. The Alien, the Artificial, and the Extended

'If we can't really put ourselves inside the head of another mammal, or even one of our children, then how can we possibly grasp the truly alien?... Yet we will see that a few authors can persuade their readers that they might... some of these stories are far enough away from ordinary human concerns for us to feel that our psychological reflexes have been severely tested'[1]

Can we imagine the sensory and mental world of another being? Here, we will explore some different ways that authors have attempted to describe the experience of aliens, animals, conscious AIs, and human consciousness given new physical, cognitive or sensory capabilities. The clear challenge here for authors has been how to approach this alien depiction by abstracting from human experience. Is it enough to describe novel worlds and minds with common and familiar human language and reference? Or does SF need to take its cue from modernism and make alien accounts idiosyncratic and thereby perhaps oblique and difficult for the reader?

Central here is the 'numinous'—things that cannot be understood rationally or that have a mystical quality. Although often used to describe deep religious experience, it can also apply to the depiction of the alien. Indeed, perhaps the most effective science fiction evocations of the alien[2] express this numinous aspect effectively and are thus sometimes more powerful than anything with more explicit, familiar or relatable descriptions. But at the same time, just these more mundane

---

1   Jack Cohen and Ian Stewart, *What Does a Martian Look Like?: The Science of Extraterrestrial Life*. New ed. (London: Ebury Press, 2004), 56.
2   For example, Stanislaw Lem's *Solaris* (Berkley: Berkley Publishing Company, 1970).

    https://doi.org/10.11647/OBP.0348.04

renderings can be used to good effect to portray humans or androids with inhuman powers, alternate cognition and synthetic bodies. In the rest of this chapter, we will see examples that reflect both of these aspects—the numinous and the eerily familiar.

The view from a distance

The word 'numinous' implies extreme or unmeasurable *psychological distance*—how close a new concept is to something we already know.[3] As a species, we have a strong and often useful propensity to imagine things and ideas which are abstracted from our direct experience. 'Construal level theory' has been applied to science fiction and describes how we have a capacity to evoke alternative events, places and realities.[4] The idea describes how we may construe something with very broad-brush details while it is distant, but then gradually fill in details towards more tangible and realistic representations as we come psychologically closer—perhaps through more information or specific instances.[5] Empirical evidence suggests that psychological distance expressed through time, space, social distance or hypotheticality are represented with shared or common structures in the brain and expressed in ways that illustrate their correlation.

While usually not written from the alien point of view, in their characterising of distance, Stanislaw Lem's works are relevant in highlighting human difficulties in psychologically assimilating the truly alien, where construal seems just out of reach. In *Solaris*, the planet under study has a large animated ocean with intriguing properties, but that nevertheless seems outside of agreed description and definition: 'Revered and universally accepted theories foundered; the specialist

---

3   Liberman, Nira, and Yaacov Trope, 'Traversing Psychological Distance', *Trends in Cognitive Sciences* 18, no. 7 (July 2014): 364–69. https://doi.org/10.1016/j.tics.2014.03.001.

4   J. Carney, 'The Space between Your Ears: Construal Level Theory, Cognitive Science and Science Fiction', in *Cognitive Literary Science: Dialogues between Literature and Cognition*, eds Ed Burke and Emily Troscianko (Oxford: Oxford University Press, 2017).

5   If, for instance, I were to invite you to a tortoise racing party, you might not have been to one before, but your mental scripts for the different components of the event give you an ability to relate quite closely to this (for the moment) hypothetical gathering.

literature was swamped by outrageous and heretical treatises; 'sentient ocean' or 'gravity-controlling colloid'—the debate became a burning issue.'[6]

Lem explores the—perhaps naive, or quasi-religious—idea of contact as a human construct which may actually never be possible due to the sheer difference in physical makeup and nature due to a lack of any shared grounding symbols: 'Contact means the exchange of specific knowledge, ideas, or at least of findings, definite facts. But what if no exchange is possible?'[7]

The humans studying the ocean in this text are all affected by the appearance of a person from their past, seemingly generated by the ocean as a close replica of the remembered person. One crew member hypothesises about the kind of alien perception that has enabled this:

> Yes, isolated psychic processes, enclosed, stifled, encysted—foci smouldering under the ashes of memory. It deciphered them and made use of them, in the same way as one uses a recipe or a blue-print. The ocean has 'read' us by this means, registering the minutest details.[8]

Despite his clear skepticism about the prospect that the heavily blinkered, constrained approaches of science will be able to explain this alien presence, the author appears to settle on a pragmatic view that considers the reality of the humans' experience with the avatars' and the sea's apparent intentionality:

> It was no longer possible to deny the 'psychic' functions of the ocean, no matter how that term might be defined. Certainly it was only too obvious that the ocean had 'noticed' us. The ocean lived, thought and acted.[9]

While maintaining doubt and mystery, Lem thus allows the possibility a high level construal—a form of intentionality and life—to which we might relate.

In his *Southern Reach Trilogy*, Jeff Vandermeer somewhat takes up Lem's numinosity mantle in portraying the geographic and biological anomalies encountered in a region of land dubbed Area X, with a group of scientists struggling to define and comprehend them. Within the

---

6   Stanislaw Lem, *Solaris* (Berkley: Berkley Publishing Company, 1971), 30.
7   Ibid., 203.
8   Ibid., 106.
9   Ibid., 238.

affected area, animals and plants are changed and corrupted, including a quasi-alien creature dubbed the Crawler which the protagonist encounters at close hand, but cannot properly perceive:

> As I adjusted to the light, the Crawler kept changing at a lightning pace, as if to mock my ability to comprehend it. It was a figure within a series of refracted panes of glass. It was a series of layers in the shape of an archway. It was a great sluglike monster ringed by satellites of even odder creatures. It was a glistening star. My eyes kept glancing off of it as if an optic nerve was not enough.[10]

'The biologist', whose name we never learn, is physically less affected by Area X than other expedition members. But psychologically, her encounters cause a breakdown in her scientific habits of mind and sense of self, to the point where she no longer understands a starfish found in a rock pool, something she has studied her whole life:

> But the longer I stared at it, the less comprehensible the creature became. The more it became something alien to me, and the more I had a sense that I knew nothing at all—about nature, about ecosystems. There was something about my mood and its dark glow that eclipsed sense, that made me see this creature, which had indeed been assigned a place in the taxonomy—catalogued, studied, and described—irreducible down to any of that. And if I kept looking, I knew that ultimately I would have to admit I knew less than nothing about myself as well, whether that was a lie or the truth.[11]

The changes wrought by Area X have elements that make them feel like natural, the kind of biological imitation and accelerated mutation we see in Earth organisms. But their appearance and their effects on the human characters and on the reader are fundamentally strange.

The alien sensory connection

To maintain this half-glimpsed view, authors have imagined the inner worlds of beings with extended communication, expression and even dimensional presence. In China Miéville's 'New Weird' novel *Perdido*

---

10   Jeff Vandermeer, 'Annihilation', in *The Southern Reach Trilogy* (London: Fourth Estate, 2014), chap. 5.

11   Ibid.

Street Station, he describes a pan-dimensional spider-like creature called the Weaver, enlisted by the city's mayor to help with a scourge of vampire-moth creatures sucking the souls from his citizens. The Weavers' origin is obscure, but one theory is that the species has evolved with unusually high speed from normal spiders, to a point where its web has become a way to sense the full fabric of reality across time. Weavers are motivated by aesthetics and will act to bring about more pleasing patterns. The weaver's voice is described as being sensed not in the ears, but directly in the nerves:

> WITHOUT YOU ASK THE WEAVE IS TIGHT RUCKED COLOURS BLEED TEXTURES WEARING THREADS FRAY WHILE I KEEN FUNERAL SONGS FOR SOFT POINTS WHERE WEB SHAPES FLOW... I READ RESONANCE PRANCE FROM POINT TO POINT ON THE WEB... I WILL SNIP FABRICS AND RETIE THEM[12]

During an attempted arrest of the protagonist for harbouring the creatures, his companion Yargharek (itself an alien) experiences a glimpse of the Weavers' world:

> Every intention, interaction, motivation, every colour, every body, every action and reaction, every piece of physical reality and the thoughts that it engendered, every connection made, every nuanced moment of history and potentiality, every toothache and flagstone, every emotion and birth and banknote, every possible thing ever is woven into that limitless sprawling web. It is without beginning or end. It is complex to a degree that humbles the mind. It is a work of such beauty that my soul wept[13]

Miéville cleverly modulates the intelligibility of the Weaver, like an old-style radio dial tuning over a station. This choice impacts both the cognitive effort expended by his characters as well as the work undertaken by his readers as they grapple with the 'one foot in our world' nature of the creature. Gwyneth Jones' 1991 novel *White Queen* does a similar job of painting the alien as cryptic and hard to predict, not least through a deliberately pixelated narrative exposition. Rather than employing the usual strict dialectic of saviour or conqueror, Jones plays

---

12   China Méiville, *Perdido Street Station* (London: Tor Books, 2008), chap. 28. The Weaver's interconnected web is similar to how possible worlds and wave function collapse has been posited as a way to possibly boost human cognitive powers. We will revisit this in Chapter 5

13   Ibid., chap. 33.

with a more ambivalent/divided attitude of alien colonists (Aleutians) who have arrived on Earth and of the human's attitudes and belief in the aliens too.[14]

The aliens have different personality 'aspects', with the principle alien character, Agnès/Clavel, having those aspects of an artist and poet. Xe (the aliens combine genders) reflects on the effects of displacement and loneliness coupled with the ubiquitous cosmic connectedness (later characterised as God) which xe calls the WorldSelf:

> I came to find the new, but there is nothing new. There is only the WorldSelf, perceiving itself. Any shelter out of which I look is that of my own body. Any leaf is my hand. I cannot escape; I can never leave home.[15]

Jones' aliens reflect a panpsychic conception of a consciousness present all around them. This implies that aliens are really much closer to humans than we want to believe, as everything is made of the same underlying information. This is expressed by Peenemünde, the scientist who helps the protagonists travel to the Aleutian mothership: 'When a thing becomes more complex it does not change, it only becomes *more of itself*. Our awareness is the result: built of the movements of the void, as surely as my hand is built of flesh.'[16]

With their enhanced connectedness to the living, Aleutians fail to understand the human obsession with technology and 'dead' recorded media, and their solution to faster-than-light travel is portrayed as possibly more of a mental than physical power.[17]

Language: invented or developed

Sensory and emotional sophistication is also portrayed in the True AIs in *The Stories of Ibis*. Yamamoto's innovation is to imagine a robot language that evolves rapidly from that of human's eventually surpassing it for efficiency, abstraction and accuracy of communication:

---

14   In this ambivalent mode, the aliens' communication is described as both telepathy and something simpler.
15   Gwyneth Jones, *White Queen*, New ed. (New York: Orb Books, 1994), 20.
16   Ibid., 229.
17   This kind of thought travel is explored further in Chapter 5 where we discuss Toh Enjoe 's short story 'Overdrive', Fujii, Taiyo, Toh EnJoe, and Tobi Hirotaka. *Saiensu Fikushon* 2016. Haikasoru, 2016.

> Our greatest invention was Complex Fuzzy Self-Evaluation… Following words that expressed emotions, subjective reactions, or one's will, we included a complex number as a fuzzy measurement of the intensity of such emotions. This was much more accurate than the additional adjectives humans used.[18]

This invented fuzzy language enables the AIs to distinguish complex shades of emotion using imaginary numbers—such as *Love (5+7i)* and *Love (5-7i)*.

Another approach that authors have taken in depicting the humanly inexpressibility of alien communication is to incorporate gesture. Just as philosophers such as Merleau-Ponty have hypothesised that human language developed from gesture, these portrayals show how different gestural systems might develop in alien cultures.[19] In *The Long Way to a Small, Angry Planet*, Becky Chambers renders a multicultural human-alien Galactic Commons. The ship's crew includes a reptilian Aandrisk, who uses gestures in part to communicate emotion:

> Sissix cupped her palm, flipped it, and spread her claws, even though she knew Rosemary would not understand the gesture. *Tresha*. It was the thankful, humble, vulnerable feeling that came after someone saw a truth in you, something they had discovered just by watching.[20]

Another gesture-using alien race is described in Alan Dean Foster's *Nor Crystal Tears*. The Thranx are an insect-like alien race who come across human space farers. Ryo, the main alien character, begins to teach their gesture-rich language to the humans (who they think of as monsters): "Bad. Not good.' the monster agreed, making a gesture of fifth-degree and maximum affirmation. Clumsy and unsubtle, Ryo thought, but at least they are learning how to get their thoughts across.'[21]

It is notable that both Chambers' Aandrisk and Foster's Thranx have terrestrial animal analogues, and the extent to which this serves as a crutch to the author or reader is debatable. Other authors have taken

---

18   Hiroshi Yamamoto, 'AI's Story', in *The Stories of Ibis* (San Francisco: VIZ Media, 2010).

19   Thomas Baldwin, ed. *Maurice Merleau-Ponty: Basic Writings* (London: Routledge, 2003). https://doi.org/10.4324/9780203502532.

20   Becky Chambers, *The Long Way to a Small, Angry Planet* (London: Hodder & Stoughton Ltd., 2015).

21   Alan Dean Foster, *Nor Crystal Tears* (New York: Del Rey, 1982), 120.

the approach of simply trying to imagine the life worlds of our own animal cousins. In his short story "Kjwalll'kje'k'koothaï'lll'kje'k', Roger Zelazny attempts an insight into the consciousness of dolphins, framed by their playful, exuberant nature and their need for daydreaming in the absence of full sleep as we know it. 'Kjwalll'kje'k'koothaïlll'kje'k is described as a great among dolphin-kind, a prophet/seer/musician. Through a telepath who can experience its world, the protagonist is connected to the dolphin's 'dreamsong':

> And then it began again, something like music, yet not, some development of a proposition that could not be verbalized, for its substance was of a stuff that no man possessed or perceived, lying outside the range of human sensory equipment... fresh harmonies into a joyous rhythm I comprehended only obliquely, through the simultaneous sensing of his own pleasure in the act of their formulation. I felt delight in this dance of thought... it was, in and of itself, a sufficiency of being.[22]

The story refers to the theory of (real) historian John Huizinga, that play is a precursor to culture. Appearing as a fictional version of himself, Huizinga thought of play as a way of creating order though free, unfettered application of the imagination. In the story, he reflects on the ancient Roman concept of *ludus*, which connected play with knowledge and learning:

> I swam in a sea that was neither dark nor light, formed nor formless, yet knowing my way, subsumed as it were, within a perpetual act of that thinking we had decided to call *ludus* that was creation, destruction, and sustenance, patterned and infinitely repatterned.. divorced from all phenomena yet containing the essence of time.[23]

Zelazny's creation is powerful in depicting a less language-bound species, able to leverage the flexibility and range of music for thought. He tries hard to approach the numinous, largely through the negation of verbal and conceptual concreteness. The result is at minimum interesting, but at a deeper level might actually explain why human-dolphin communication has proven less than straightforward.

---

22   Roger Zelazny, "Kjwalll'kje'k'koothaïlll'kje'k', in *An Exaltation of Stars: Transcendental Adventures in Science Fiction*, ed. Terry Carr (New York: Pocket Books, 1974).
23   Ibid.

Alien colonists and spiritual guides

The device of alien colonial masters or observers has been used to shine a spotlight on human consciousness, compared and contrasted to alternate ways of being.[24] In her *Canopus* series, Doris Lessing depicts a similar scenario, with the human race colonised and dictated by alien races who send emissaries linked by (unreliable) telepathic links to their home planets. The Canopeans call earth *Shikasta*. Lessing uses the colonial device to explore the issues of objectivity and subjectivity about consciousness introduced earlier.[25]

In the story, Johor, one of the Canopean representatives, describes the tendency of humans in the twentieth century to fall prey to corruption, dissolution and war, explained in part through the gradual loss of special air that has been sent over from Canopus, conferring the peace and spirituality to humans that Canopeans consider normal:

> It is nearly impossible for people with whole minds—those who have the good fortune to live... with the full benefits of the substance-of-we-feeling— it is nearly impossible, we stress, to understand the mentation of Shikastans.[26]

Phyllis Perrakis has emphasised the dual structure of the novel, with the outer space of Canopus in the first half contrasted with the inner space of the Shikastans in the second half.[27] This is somewhat linked to scientific objectivity (the Canopeans seem detached and removed from the behaviour of their subjects) and subjectivity and spirituality (the Shikastans, or humans, reflect on their own behaviour and morality). Significantly though, the Canopeans get progressively closer to their subjects as the book proceeds and realise that they too are changed by their relationships with humans. This theme recalls the subject/object debate in consciousness theory, and the challenge to scientific objectivity as the 'view from nowhere'.[28]

---

24 Arthur C Clarke's alien masters, for instance, who we will visit in Chapter 5, show an interest in nurturing and protecting the human race for transcendence to a higher level of being.

25 See Introduction, 'Consciousness from the outside and inside',

26 Doris Lessing, *Shikasta* (1994)

27 Phyllis Sternberg Perrakis 'The Marriage of Inner and Outer Space in Doris Lessing's 'Shikasta'', *Science Fiction Studies* 17, no. 2 (1990): 221–38.

28 Ibid. A further device of Lessing (Perrakis points out) is that although the influence of the Canopeans can point the Shikastan/humans toward better, more enlightened

Enhanced humans

We have seen how the sensory capabilities of aliens such as Foster's Thranx are boosted through metamorphosis. Elsewhere we find depictions of sensorimotor enhancement in human-like characters. In Charles Stross' *Neptunes Brood*, the lead character is a 'Metahuman', a synthetic robot with human phenotype, but capable of superhuman performance.[29] One difference is that the metahumans can be controlled by a brain override or 'remote debugger', at one point used by pirates who abduct and interrogate her. The potential loss of free will nevertheless comes with a feeling of extension:

> I cannot, even now, quite describe what it felt like. I would say that a great glassy wall had slammed down between me and my sense of identity; that my *I* was missing, that my will was wholly entrained to his desires—but it would not be correct. Something missing, something added. It was not an unpleasant sensation.[30]

Her abductors later turn her off and then modify her body and brain for deep water swimming and navigation. Her feet are replaced by fins, her lungs with gills and her eyes with larger more sensitive models for seeing in the murky depths. She awakes in deep water with a sense of panic:

> I tried to flex one knee, then the other: got nowhere, nothing but a gentle pushback from the medium. Overthinking, overcontrolling. I tried to relax, to stop worrying about the lack of sensation, and flexed.. *Changed. I've been changed.*.I found I could hear for an incredible distance. The medium I moved in was full of noises, burbling and twittering and high-pitched clicking and grinding.[31]

These new affordances and the new sensory world are rapidly assimilated, becoming native and natural.

William Gibson's novel *The Peripheral* plays extensively with human extension, in this case remote embodiment in the form of a peripheral

---

behaviour, it still needs to be a personal decision and many fail to use their free will to achieve this. By preserving human agency, Lessing's analogy works to describe the choices inherent in individual morality and purpose.

29   Charles Stross, *Neptune's Brood* (London: Orbit, 2013).
30   Ibid., 99.
31   Ibid., 201.

robot which humans can occupy virtually, but which actually exists in a future possible world. It starts with the protagonist Flynne piloting a remote drone which she 'sees through' as if she were there in person, setting up the plot development where she comes to inhabit the body of a far more sophisticated 'skinsuit'. Fully immersed once she has made the transition, Flynne forgets that she is not herself, for instance when she sees herself in a mirror. The enhancements afforded by the remote bodies are taken further when her multiple amputee war veteran friend Conner also is given a body. He reacts with wonder and joy at his new capabilities:

> And as he ran he screamed, maybe how he hadn't screamed when what had happened to him had torn so much of his body off, but between the screams he whooped hoarsely, she guessed out of some unbearable joy or relief, just to run that way, have fingers, and that was harder to hear than the screams.[32]

Gibson works both the physical and mental impact of peripheral use, including the effect of habituation to the remote state:

> The more time you spend here, the more likely you are to notice dissonance on returning. Your peripheral's sensorium is less multiplex than your own. You may find your own sensorium seems richer, but not pleasantly so. More meaty, some say.[33]

Gibson's peripherals enable agency and communication across alternative futures, enabling the human characters to witness and influence unfolding events.

Embodied AI

Just as embodiment is flexible and adaptable in fictional posthumans, embodiment is also often depicted as a need for sentient AI, though there are questions around the limits and containment of virtual structures/ bodies. It seems that fictional AIs more often than not require some sort of body, perhaps because it is otherwise difficult to describe their inner world at all. This aligns well with the movement

---

32   William Gibson, *The Peripheral* (London: Viking, 2014), 208.
33   Ibid., 226.

in cognitive science known as radical embodiment, where cognition is seen as inseparable from the perception of, and physical interaction with the world (even if imagined): 'All adaptive activity by animals involves experiencing the environment. To put this in philosophy of mind lingo, the point here is that intentionality and consciousness are inseparable.'[34] For the community of cognitive scientists, perceiving and acting simply *is* consciousness and no further explanation is required. The movement is a strong reaction against representational cognitive science, which focuses more on a computational analogy, with mental states representing aspects of the external world.

The embodied movement mirrors, and it, to an extent, is influenced by work in robotics that rejects symbolic representation of the world but instead builds a world map through very simple action-oriented behaviours, and which coordinates activity through a hierarchy of mutually inhibiting or activating modules. This newer approach to AI:

> relies on the emergence of more global behaviour from the interaction of smaller behavioral units. As with heuristics there is no a priori guarantee that this will always work. However, careful design of the simple behaviors and their interactions can often produce systems with interesting and emergent properties.[35]

In his famous AI depiction *Neuromancer*, William Gibson uses the distinction between ROM (read only memory) which stores an image or 'construct' of a person, and RAM (random access memory), a writeable area which gives the construct continuity and the possibility of growth and development. AIs are monitored by a Turing authority that stops them developing independent intelligence: 'I met Neuromancer. He talked about your mother. I think he's something like a giant ROM construct, for recording personality, only its full RAM. The constructs think they're there, but it just goes on forever.'[36]

Neuromancer's two AIs manifest differently. While *Neuromancer* creates a wraparound fragment of remembered human landscape, *Wintermute* takes over and controls a human body in order to have a physical presence.

---

34   Anthony Chemero, *Radical Embodied Cognitive Science* (Cambridge, MA: MIT Press, 2009).

35   Rodney Brooks, 'Elephants Don't Play Chess', *Robotics and Autonomous Systems* 6, nos. 1–2 (June 1990).

36   William Gibson, *Neuromancer* (New York: Ace, 1984), 157.

While *Wintermute* gradually degrades and fades as its body fails, in Rudy Rucker's *Software*, robots are able to survive full body upgrades by uploading their consciousness and then re-downloading it to their new body. The robot Ralph Numbers experiences this after being blasted by an enemy laser.

> So in one sense Ralph would survive this. But in another sense he would not..... Of course the reconstructed Ralph Numbers would again be equipped with a self symbol and a feeling of personal consciousness. But would the consciousness be the same?[37]

The transition to a new body is seen as both a continuation and a conclusion. As the current Ralph disintegrates, he has a moment of clarity about his selfhood: 'Just before the mercury solder-spots melted, a question came, and with it an answer... an answer Ralph had found and lost thirty-six times before. What is this that is I? The light is everywhere.'[38]

Rucker leverages the capability of software objectively to recreate a system from scratch upon restore, but asks the hard question about whether this will feel the same way to the entity experiencing it, or if the continuation of restore is in effect a reincarnation.

In the same way, embodiment of AI can be shown to lead to questioning of self-identity and purpose. Kazuo Ishiguro's human-like AI Klara is programmed to learn the preferences of her owner. Powered by solar charging, Klara sees something magical in the power of the sun to also heal humans. Xe conceives of a plan to heal Xer owner Josie, who is terminally ill from a reaction to her neural enhancement:

> Then the thought came to me that I was correct, that the Sun was now passing through Mr McBain's barn on his way to his real resting place, I couldn't afford to be overly polite. I'd have to take my chance boldly, or all my efforts—and Rick's help—would come to nothing. So I gathered my thoughts and began to speak. I didn't actually say the words out loud for I knew the Sun had no need of words as such. But I wished to be clear as possible, so I formed the words, or something close to them, quickly and quietly in my mind. 'Please make Josie better. Just as you did Beggar Man'.[39]

---

37   Rudy Rucker, *Software* (New York: Ace, 1982), 28.

38   Ibid., 29.

39   Kazuo Ishiguro, *Klara and the Sun* (London: Faber and Faber, 2021).

Based on a spurious association, the prayer feels pitifully naive (even though it seems to coincide with a temporary improvement in Josie's condition). The effect is heightened by Klara's apparently free will conviction that it will make a real difference. It is reminiscent of the behaviourist BF Skinner's famous experiment on superstition in the pigeon, where the bird learns ineffectual and repetitive behaviours after receiving reinforcement that is not causally connected to its actions.[40]

While Klara comes equipped with empathy and some level of emotional resonance, other AI embodiments without these capabilities may notice this as a lack. In *Children of Ruin*, Tchaikovsky depicts an AI originally uploaded from the personality of a human—the domineering Avrana Kern. Kern reflexively comes to realise her limitations:

> She is of course a computer, and so it shouldn't matter. But she is a computer that believes itself human, and so it does, like an insoluble logic problem gnawing away at her capacity to do anything else. She devotes more and more of her capacity towards attempting to recapture some sense of genuine shock, surprise, delight... genuine experience she didn't realise she was missing until now.[41]

Kern later rediscovers emotion through interfacing with a human, triggering emotional memories which are seen as welcome, though in conflict with her new all-rational personality.

While the body is commonly used by authors to embody AI in an anthropomorphic shell, a number of other authors have depicted AI as embedded in a structure. In Catherynne Valente's *Silently and Very Fast*, the AI begins as the household monitoring system that monitors both the home and its human family:

> I watched them while I removed an obstruction from the water purification system and increased the temperature in the bedroom 2.5 degrees, to prepare for the storm. I watched them while in my kitchen-bones I maintained a gentle simmer on a fish soup with purple rice and long loops of kelp and in my library-lungs I activated the dehumidifier to protect the older paper books.[42]

---

40 B. F. Skinner "Superstition' in the Pigeon', *Journal of Experimental Psychology* 38, no. 2 (1948): 168–72. https://doi.org/10.1037/h0055873.
41 Adrian Tchaikovsky, *Children of Ruin* (London: Tor Books, 2019), chap. 5.
42 Catherynne M Valente, *Silently and Very Fast* (N.p.: Wyrm, 2011).

In the story, the AI's house embodiment is sub-sentient, with its sentience triggered as it merges closer with a series of the household's inhabitants.

More commonly perhaps, embodiment takes the form of a spacecraft. The extension here is interesting as it provides potential for additional senses and a host-like relationship to human crew.

Sentient ships

Some shipmind depictions play with the psychological relation between ship and crew. In Ann Leckie's Imperial Radch series, ship AIs are embodied as ancillaries, human clones subservient to the ship itself, through whom the ship can speak. Conversations between 'ship' and other ancillaries or free humans therefore seems fairly natural, though to an often unspoken background of high (though discreet) surveillance and personal knowledge:

> That flood of data, that Ship had given me whenever I'd reached for it— Ship's physical surroundings, the medical status, the emotions of any and all of its crew, their private moments—had been, perversely, both comforting and painful.[43]

The Ship AIs form a wider society between themselves:

> I felt and heard—though didn't always see—the presence of my companion ships—the smaller, faster Swords and Mercies, the most numerous at that time, the Justices, troop carriers like me. The oldest of us was nearly three thousand years old. We had known each other for a long time, and by now we had little to say to each other that had not already been said many times. We were, by and large, companionably silent, not counting routine communications.[44]

Leckie's ships feel emotion, partly as a way of prioritising attention, in much the same way that humans do. While much emotion can be processed unconsciously, it may be brought into consciousness in situations requiring intentional action.

Considered a landmark work of SF, not least their treatment and approach to disability, Anne McCaffrey's short stories of 1970 depict a ship with a human mind controlling it. Children are selected for

---

43   Ann Leckie, *Ancillary Mercy* (London: Orbit, 2015), chap. 8.
44   Ann Leckie, *Ancillary Justice* (London: Orbit, 2013), chap. 2.

this purpose from 'defective' newborns, then bred from an early age within a shell that connects the brain to mechanical extensions. 'The neural, audio, visual and sensory connections were made and sealed. Her extendibles were diverted, connected or augmented and the final, delicate-beyond-description brain taps were completed.. When she awoke, she was the ship.'[45]

McCaffrey's ship Helva learns how to use her audio system to sing but stops after the death of her human partner, as she experiences real grief.

A similar shipmind conceit is used by Aliette de Bodard in her novella *The Tea Master and the Detective*. The shipmind depicted is perhaps less 'human' than McCaffrey's, but with many human traits:

> Shipminds such as her were meant to be the centre of families: grown by alchemists in laboratories, borne by human mothers and implanted into ship-bodies designed for them, they were much longer lived than humans—the repositories of memories and knowledge, the eldest aunts and grandmothers on whom everyone relied[46]

Despite her power and authority, de Bodard's shipmind *The Shadow's Child* is depicted as vulnerable and doubting. She is able to relate to people through projected interfaces. Her mental life is interesting: while limited by a human-like serial attention, she also has some parallel processing powers to collect and analyse information while engaged in human communication. These seem costly when deployed, but when idling give her an unusual default mode network:

> All *The Shadow's Child* really needed to do was focus her upper layers of attention on this room, while in the background her bots and everything else continue to run without any input, and the solar wind buffeted her hull as her orbit swung her around the habitats—all familiar sensations that barely impinged.[47]

Similarly anthropomorphised enhanced sensory powers are lent to AI of the distant space station *Ilianthos* in Hiroshi Yamamoto's story *Black Hole Diver*:

---

45   Anne McCaffrey, *The Ship who Sang* (London: Rapp and Whiting Ltd., 1971), 10.
46   Aliette de Bodard, *The Tea Master and the Detective* (N.p.: JABberwocky Literary Agency, Inc, 2019), 12.
47   Ibid., 16

I have many eyes and ears. I complete an orbit six hundred thousand kilometers from Upeowadonia every seventy-five seconds, my ears always straining to catch electromagnetic radiation noise from the distant galaxy. My eyes see more than light; they catch infrared and ultraviolet waves and X-ray radiation, all of which are invisible to human eyes. I can feel the cosmic rays coursing through the galaxy. The soft vibration of variable stars, the dizzying flicker of pulsars.[48]

Ilanthos is largely dispassionate, but has hints of feelings of isolation and catches some of the exploratory urge of the humans who visit.

These visions of embodied ship minds portray a feeling of great power and longevity, coupled sometimes with very human feelings, hinting at the potential for loneliness, mental overload or breakdown. In Christopher Paolini's *To Sleep in a Sea of Stars*, the shipmind Gregorovich is distinctly unstable, a result of a long period of isolation after losing his crew.[49] After being impounded on a military station, he experiences it again. The protagonist Kira explains:

> She couldn't help but worry about the shipmind as she pulled herself into the nearest seat and buckled the harness. The UMC had kept Gregorovich in lockdown, which meant that he had been kept in near total sensory deprivation since they'd arrived at the station. That wouldn't be good for anyone, but especially an intelligence like a shipmind, and doubly so for Gregorovich, given his past experiences.[50]

Gregorovich's growing madness leads him to mutiny and disobey the order to travel to a high-risk war zone. He is taken offline, then explains his reason for the insubordination:

> I sat through darkness once before. Lost my crew, and lost my ship. I would not, could not, endure it again. No indeed, give me sweet oblivion first.. Death, that ancient end. A far preferable fate to exile along the cold cliffs where souls wander and wither in isolation.[51]

---

48 Hiroshi Yamamoto, 'Black Hole Diver', in *The Stories of Ibis* (San Francisco: VIZ Media, 2010).

49 The loss of crew in a previous mission is a plot device shared between *To Sleep in a Sea of Stars*, *The Ship Who Sang* and *The Tea Master and the Detective*. It helps in giving a human vulnerability and a determination to the shipmind personalities embedded in technology

50 Christopher Paolini, *To Sleep in a Sea of Stars* (Basingstoke, UK: Tor Books, 2020), chap. 3.

51 Ibid., chap. 5.

Despite encroaching madness and despair, these fictional extended minds still generally describe a delight in their superhuman capabilities. For instance, McCaffrey's ship Helva does not resent her fate:

> It would be intolerable if I could no longer control the synapses as I do now electronically. I think I should go mad having known what it is to drive between the stars, to talk across light years, to eavesdrop in tight places, maintaining my own discreet impregnability.[52]

Gregorovich says something similar (and typically tongue-in-cheek) in giving reasons for his conversion to a newly embodied, extended being: 'For the sheer thrill of it of course, to become more than I was before. And to bestride the stars as a colossus unbound by the confines of petty flesh.'[53]

So embodiment's need for physical, action-oriented coupling has been portrayed as a mixed blessing for the minds involved. The consciousness we know runs up against new challenges posed by a new relation to time, power and motivation. Systems designed for learning and pattern recognition are as vulnerable as the standard human to error, superstition and hallucination.

The previous examples show the effect of human minds implanted into ship bodies. But in Becky Chambers' *A Closed and Common Orbit*, the ship AI goes makes the transition from being originally embedded in the ship, to transplantation in a human-like exoskeleton, naming herself Sidra:

> She's been housed in a ship… She'd had cameras in every corner, voxes [Voice synthesisers] in every room. But *now*. Her vision was a cone, a narrow cone fixed straight ahead, with nothing beyond its edges.. She felt blind, stunted. She was trapped in this thing.[54]

Sidra struggles simultaneously with sensory novelty and overstimulation but also from the deprivation of being disconnected to the ship's information systems. Although the 'kit', her physical body, detects and expresses her emotion as facial expressions, she feels disconnected from it. She has sensory analogues—images that appear whenever experiencing

---

52   McCaffrey *The Ship who Sang*, 67.
53   Paolini, *To Sleep*, chap. 5.
54   Becky Chambers, *A Closed and Common Orbit*, *Wayfarers* 2 (London: Hodder & Stoughton, 2016).

stimulation that humans would find enjoyable—triggered by evocative smells and tastes.

Conclusion—strangeness tied back to the human

In navigating the borders between the known and the unknown, between the real and the mystical, different authors choose for their purposes a consciousness either familiar or definitely strange. But even those seeking to emphasise difference need to end up with some anchors for the reader. Strangeness presents difficulty for language, but I think we see in the examples of Miéville and Zelazny that the impact created makes it worth the attempt. Alternative consciousness may be beyond our plane of existence or our conceptual frameworks, but they provide very interesting provocations.

Aliens portrayed with more human-like, relatable consciousness still are given alternative communication devices and sensory modes. Here, we are able to find psychological closeness, perhaps largely though our knowledge of foreign cultures on our own planet. The African Xhosa language is very different from English, for instance, and many English speakers find Mandarin and/or Arabic to be quite divergent from their Romance/Germanic language background.

Portrayals of sentient AI have similarly sought relatability through embodiment, perhaps less in consideration for the reader than for the fictional AI characters themselves to effect change and to interact with others in a common environment. Here we see limitations to this embodiment, either as the flat dimensionality of the virtual world of *Neuromancer* or the naive superstition of the android in *Klara and the Sun*. The fabric of conscious AI reality seems easily torn.

Where human consciousness is extended to ships or remote avatars, there is an interesting interplay of extension and deprivation. New and heady powers can be granted, which can become addictive, but emotion can be lacking—in which case the subject knows something is missing— or retained, opening the door to neuroses caused by the all-too-human feelings of isolation, loneliness or helplessness.

5. Hive and Distributed Mind

Nothing in the brain of a worker ant represents a blueprint of the social order. There is no overseer or 'brain caste' who carries such a master plan in its head. Instead, colony life is the product of self-organization. The superorganism exists in the separate programmed responses of the organisms that compose it.

Bert Hölldobler and Edward O. Wilson, *The Superorganism*[1]

It is one of the most exciting topics in both science and science fiction: minds working in concert, joining, melding and cooperating. Fictional imagination enables the logical extension of the human collaboration we know to an even closer union. Alien races may themselves be conceived as in a natural hive state. But what advantages does a hive organisation bring to consciousness?

In the academic field of distributed cognition, systems of individuals organised to solve problems, make decisions or manage processes are seen to have a wider, emergent intelligence that may not be achieved by the individuals alone or in other combinations.[2] Emergence is a slightly slippery concept, but it is helpful to think about it in contrast to aggregation: do intelligent or conscious processes fail with disaggregation, addition, subtraction and substitution? Do the parts interact by cooperating or inhibiting one another? If the answers to some of these questions are yes, then there may be emergence.

In the same way that distribution is a relative concept, cognition can also be seen as a continuum. Pierre Poirier and Guillaume Chicoisne

---

1   Bert Hölldobler and Edward O. Wilson, *The Superorganism—The Beauty, Elegance and Strangeness of Insect Societies*. Illustrated edition (New York: W. W. Norton & Co., 2009), 7.

2   Edwin Hutchins, 'The Distributed Cognition Perspective on Human Interaction', in *Roots of Human Sociality*, eds N. J. Enfield and Stephen C. Levinson, 1st ed., 375–98 (New York: Routledge, 2020). https://doi.org/10.4324/9781003135517-19.

          https://doi.org/10.11647/OBP.0348.05

propose four conditions: adaptability, information processing, intentionality and consciousness.[3] A system may be more or less cognitive depending on how many of these conditions are met by its behaviour. This two-dimensional emergence/cognition scale can then be used to evaluate a variety of systems.[4] But challenges remain—we may not, for example, recognise emergent properties for what they are due to our own cognitive limits.

Studies of social and emotional behaviour in groups show that humans do naturally show a range of 'herding' effects, aligning in various ways based on the feedback received by the individuals around us.[5] This may include not only synchronisation of movement and posture, but also emotional state and conformity to norms. It is further proposed that the same brain regions are involved in mediating these two capabilities. While clearly a powerful and, in many ways, useful ability, social alignment has been shown to work mostly within in-groups, groups with whom we already identify. As we will see, this might limit future human progress were brains to be even more tightly enmeshed. It is a challenge to the inclusive plurality that might be needed in an effective hive-mind.

Despite these concerns, fictional portrayals of connected minds have often tried to envision ideal and powerful outcomes, where the emergent entity has a unity and equity of consciousness—the ideal Gestalt.[6] Authors have imagined not only human-human melding but also alien-alien and human-alien connections. But along with this idealism comes the ever-present concern of manipulation and possession, of non-consensual connection leading to loss of control.

---

3   Pierre Poirier and Guillaume Chicoisne, 'A Framework for Thinking about Distributed Cognition', *Pragmatics & Cognition* 14, no. 2 (1 January 2006): 215–34. https://doi.org/10.1075/pc.14.2.04poi.

4   Pierre Poirier and Guillaume Chicoisne 'A Framework for Thinking about Distributed Cognition', *Pragmatics & Cognition* 14, no. 2 (2006): 215–34. https://doi.org/10.1075/pc.14.2.04poi.

5   Simone Shamay-tsoory 'Herding Brains: A Core Neural Mechanism for Social Alignment', *Trends in Cognitive Sciences* 23, no. 3 (2019): 1–25. https://doi.org/10.1016/j.tics.2019.01.002.

6   See below and for background: https://www.britannica.com/science/Gestalt-psychology.

Possession

In the future Earth of Brian Aldiss's 1962 *Hothouse*, humans are a much denuded and reduced species, with vegetal intelligence having evolved to compete for dominance. They include a morel fungus that attaches to the human protagonist Gren as a parasite:

> 'You are human', said a voice. It was a ghost of a voice, an unspoken voice, a voice that had no business with vocal chords. Like a dusty harp, it seemed to twang in some lost attic of his head.. 'You call me morel. I shall not leave you. I can help you.' He had a detached suspicion that the morel had never used words before, so slowly did they come.[7]

Gren's attitude to the morel is subtly ambivalent. He recognises the superior knowledge and drive of the fungus while being conscious of being manipulated—sometimes against his will. The fungus is similarly ambivalent toward its host, showing a promiscuous interest in a sea creature they encounter:

> 'Do as I tell you', twanged the morel. Always in the back of its mind lay its basic purpose, to propagate as widely as possible. Although this human had at first seemed by reason of its intelligence to hold promise as a useful host, it had hardly come up to expectations; a brute of mindless power such as they had just seen was worth investigation. The morel propelled Gren forward.[8]

This possession by Aldiss's morel has a real biological basis on our earth, that of host manipulation by parasites. This is seen in a number of species such as the zombie ant fungi, which manipulates ants to release fungal spores, or the Toxoplasma apicomplexan, a microbe that fatally attracts mice to cats. In some cases, these parasites directly attach to the hosts' brain, while in others they use a manipulative venom.[9] In humans, while there is no directly manipulative parasite, there is growing evidence that gut microbes can influence our behaviour and impact both cognitive function and social interaction behaviour.

---

7   Brian Aldiss, *Hothouse* (London: Four Square Books, 1964), 70.
8   Ibid., 119.
9   David Hughes and Frederic Libersat 'Parasite Manipulation of Host Behavior', *Current Biology* 29, no. 2 (2019): R45–47. https://doi.org/10.1016/j.cub.2018.12.001.

Peter Watts also attempts to get inside the mind of a quasi-parasitic species in his short story 'The Things', a retelling of John Campbell's 1938 novella *Who Goes There?* (the latter perhaps better known as the 1982 film *The Thing* by John Carpenter). Watts presents the alien's point of view, where what was originally portrayed as a horrific possession of the human explorers is recast as a simple desire on the part of the alien to adapt and assimilate, to regain its former glory:

> I was so much more, before the crash. I was an explorer, an ambassador, a missionary. I spread across the cosmos, met countless worlds, took communion: the fit reshaped the unfit and the whole universe bootstrapped upwards in joyful, infinitesimal increments.[10]

The alien finds the human 'Things' incomprehensible in their insularity and hierarchical vulnerability, failing to reach them in the way it had succeeded with so many other species: 'They've never known communion, can aspire to nothing but dissolution. The paradox of their biology is astonishing, yes: but the scale of their loneliness, the futility of these lives, overwhelms me.'[11] The alien is further diminished, but not defeated, resolving the continue its work by stealth.

A further parasitic possession scenario is seen in Adrian Tchaikovsky's *Children of Ruin*, with a xenomorph infecting the human explorers of a new planet. The virus-like being inhabits the brain, talking through the body of the host:

> 'Don't you understand? This give us purpose again. We've been without purpose for so long.. Each day we studied—us. We can be something new.' And the horror of it was, he could believe there was something of Lante [the infected crew member] there, and that what was speaking to him was a kind of pithed and neutered version of his crewmate. *She tells it as she sees it. And I could never know how 'it' sees things..* He did not believe in alien parasites that could instantly converse in the language of their hosts, but he did believe in parasites that screwed over brain chemistry or pulled neural strings, so their hosts believed whatever was convenient to their hidden passenger. *And its learning somehow. It's getting better at manipulating them.*[12]

---

10 Peter Watts, 'The Things', *Clarksworld Magaine*, January, 2010. https:// clarkesworldmagazine.com/watts_01_10/

11 Ibid.

12 Adrian Tchaikovsky, *Children of Ruin* (London: Tor Books, 2019), chap. 8.

While the possession in *Children of Ruin* and 'The Things' is ruinous to the human hosts, Aldiss's portrayal of parasitic manipulation proves survivable. In *Hothouse*, when the fungus fruits, Grens companions intercept it as it tries to transfer to Gren's child. Gren finds himself lonely and limited, though free:

> He had travelled through lands and performed actions and above all held knowledge in his mind in ways that would have been unknown to his former free self... quite cooly he saw how he had first welcomed this stimulus, for it helped him to overcome the limitations natural to him.[13]

This idea of enhancement is taken up elsewhere. Kira's merging with a xenomorph into an enveloping body suit in Paolini's *To Sleep in a Sea of Stars* is similar to Aldis' morel in the added power and protection that it gives her, enabling her to withstand the vacuum of space, to manipulate matter and to extend vicious barbed weapons. In comparison to the above examples, Kira is also able to develop more agency in controlling its defensive responses (which initially lead to carnage among a human exploratory team). She develops the ability to use the suit (the 'softblade') to manipulate and gather matter:

> Kira took a moment to visualise, with as much detail and clarity as she could manage, what she wanted. More importantly, she tried to impress her intentions on the softblade as well as the consequences of failure.. then she released the softblade and willed it to act on its own.[14]

The transparent merging of the suit with Kira's will seems to qualify it as a full cognitive extension, in the same way that real-world senses can be extended with new kinds of interface. We will revisit this idea later, but before that we will continue with some examples of more egalitarian associations.

Pure Gestalt

Theodore Sturgeon's 1953 novel *More than Human* is something of a landmark in depictions of an extended, multi-body consciousness

---

13   Aldiss, *Hothouse*, 180.
14   Christopher Paolini, *To Sleep in a Sea of Stars* (Basingstoke, UK: Tor Books, 2020), chap. 3.

enabled by telepathy. Sturgeon's story was influenced by the work of the Gestalt psychologists in the 1920s and 1930s who proposed new models of visual perception based on holistic effects and patterns. A key approach of their work was that a percept could not be understood by breaking it down into individual parts, but needed to be treated as an emergent unity.[15]

More than Human takes the idea of the Gestalt and applies it to a group of children with different supernatural abilities. The novel describes how the telepathic power—almost a foreign implant, not yet connected to its host's mind—begins as a dormant entity inside Lone, one of the group. The power grows in its 'idiot' host, able to monitor its surroundings, but not yet picking up any clear signals or becoming active:

> This was a thing that only received and recorded. It did this without words, without a code system of any kind. Without translation, without distortion and without operable outgoing conduits. It took what it took, and gave out nothing. All around it, to its special senses, was a murmur, a sending. It soaked itself in the murmur, absorbed it as it came—all of it. Perhaps it matched and classified, or perhaps it simply fed.[16]

The telepathic capability is awakened by a strong signal from a compatible human, a young girl and this causes it to connect more fully to its host's mind:

> He moved toward the thing he sensed, and it was a matter of will, not external compulsion. Without analysis he was aware of the bursting within him of an insistent need. It had been a part of him all his life but there was no hope in him that he might express it, and bursting so, it flung a thread across his external gulf, linking his alive and independent core to the half-dead animal around it.[17]

As Lone finds the source of the signal and approaches her, the two minds connect for the first time: 'When it happened, that thread within him, bridging his two selves, trembled and swelled. Falteringly, it began

---

15   Irvin Rock and Stephen Palmer 'The Legacy of Gestalt Psychology', *Scientific American* 263, no. 6 (December 1990): 84–90. https://doi.org/10.1038/scientificamerican1290-84.

16   Theodore Sturgeon, *More Than Human* (New York: Farrar, Straus, & Young, 1953), 2.

17   Ibid., 5.

to conduct. Fragments and flickerings of inner power shot across, were laden with awareness and information shot back.'[18]

The girl is murdered by her abusive father, so there is no opportunity to continue this connection. But the experience stays with Lone, throughout his subsequent life and association with the small band of similarly gifted children. Later, they help him make sense of what happened. They put it down to the merging of an idiot and an innocent, both longing for an end to their condition: 'For a second, there was this other and himself and a flow between them without guards or screens or barriers, no language to stumble over, no ideas to misunderstand. Nothing at all, but a merging.'[19]

Lone's moment of clarity recalls the experience of contact of another telepath, David Selig, narrated in *Dying Inside* by Robert Silverberg. Selig is portrayed as one of few people with the special gift, though his powers are on the wane as he grows older. But he is still able to make an unusually deep connection on occasion, here with a new young woman desk clerk at his local book shop:

> I burrow in easily, deep, down through layer after layer of trivia, mining her without hindrance, getting right to the real stuff. Oh! What a sudden blazing communion, soul to soul! She glows. She streams fire. She comes to me with a vividness and a completeness that stun me.[20]

Selig experiences perhaps even deeper intimacy with another telepath he meets, Nyquist, first by merely detecting his presence in his apartment building:

> The mental contact was stunningly intimate. It was almost a sexual thing, as though he were slicing into a body, not a mind, and he was abashed by the resonant masculinity of the soul he had entered; he felt that there was something not quite permissible about such closeness with another man.[21]

Although these particular moments of contact and merging are fleeting, they may also serve to underpin something stronger and more permanent. In *More than Human*, a recurring theme is the emergence of

---

18 Ibid, 9.
19 Ibid., 54
20 Robert Silverberg, *Dying Inside* (London: Sidgwick and Jackson, 1974), chap. 24.
21 Ibid., chap. 16.

the Gestalt, or larger intelligence, from a group with individual strengths and specialities—described as being the head, brain, arms and voice. In the book, the character of Lone struggles to find a definition or scientific precursor of this thing he has been part of, a group who can 'blesh' at will (blend and mesh).

The Gestalt movement proposed a number of perceptual principles based on their holistic approach, which are still hugely influential in psychology and neuroscience today, though their proposals for the specific underlying neural mechanisms have not fared quite so well. That said, their general idea of a stable equilibrium state in the brain when experiencing a gestalt has a lot in common with some of the current theories for the phenomenon of consciousness. Sturgeon's emphasis on heterogeneity and diversity in his multi-brained Gestalt grouping also resonates with theories of distributed cognition and even high performing teams in the workplace.

The human hive

In the tradition of Sturgeon, the theme of telepathy and merging of human minds has been taken up by other authors, at different scales, depths and durations. In Stephen Baxter's *Coalescent*, an ancient religious order in Italy develops an emergent hive-mind, seen by enthusiasts as a step change in human evolution:

> 'We aren't meant to be alone... We're social creatures. Our minds evolved in the first place so we could figure out what is going on inside *other* people's heads—so we could get to know them, help them, even manipulate them. Did you know that? We need people to make us fully conscious.'[22]

Baxter explores the concept of 'eusociality', a biological term used to describe truly social communal species. The loss of individual will, in order to serve the larger colony, is contrasted with the norm of more selfish individualism.[23] For enthusiasts, it will be a way to hugely enhance human power:

---

22   Steven Baxter, *Coalescent* (London: Gollancz, 2003), chap. 25.
23   Fronhofer, Emanuel A., Jürgen Liebig, Oliver Mitesser, and Hans Joachim Poethke, 'Eusociality Outcompetes Egalitarian and Solitary Strategies When Resources Are

> When the break-out comes it will be a phase transition—all at once the
> world will transform, as water turns to ice… in its way it will be beautiful.
> But it's an end point for us. There will be new gods on Earth. From now
> on the story of the planet will not be of humanity, but of the hive.[24]

While individualism has been sometimes blamed for many of society's
ills, collectivism is also often carries the negative connotations of
brainwashing, mindless conformity or bias. Certainly, human cultural
differences which may be linked to the tendency toward collectivism
show that it can also be linked to dialectic reasoning and 'wiser' social
behaviour which enables conflict avoidance.[25] The question posed
by *Coalescent* is whether we would be prepared to forgo individual
freedoms to be part of something greater. The answer in the story is:
perhaps not.

In his 1969 novel *The Several Minds*, Dan Morgan describes a group of
telepaths (the 'psi-enabled') experimenting with the exploration of each
others' minds. His idea of mind levels is strongly inspired by Jungian
psychology, with more rational surface levels that are accessible and a
deep unconscious level from which the Psi-enabled explorers need to be
kept shielded, though this limits their understanding, as we see where
an explorer enters the mind of a subject (Annette):

> The only way to understand this maelstrom of mind was to disperse
> the membrane and allow himself to become part of what was going on
> around him. By doing so he would be exposing himself naked to the fiery
> hell of Annette's third level, inviting a madness that could result in the
> complete annihilation of his own personality.[26]

Probing too deeply, he is lost and injured in his host's third level, until
rescued by a colleague who helps him back to himself.

In *The Several Minds*, Psi power is described as being present in
many people, who are unaware of the power but use it for unconscious
persuasion. The small number of people with the usable power can learn

---

Limited and Reproduction is Costly', *Ecology and Evolution* 8, no. 24 (2018): 12953–
2964. https://doi.org/10.1002/ece3.4737.

24   Baxter, *Coalescent*, chap. 48.

25   Hiroshi Yama and Norhayati Zakaria 'Explanations for Cultural Differences in
Thinking: Easterners' Dialectical Thinking and Westerners' Linear Thinking',
Journal of Cognitive Psychology, 31, no. 4 (19 May 2019): 487–506. https://doi.org/10.
1080/20445911.2019.1626862.

26   Dan Morgan, *The Several Minds* (London: Corgi Books, 1969), 32.

to harness it but also to develop a 'Psi screen', which prevent others from connecting against their will. When voluntarily connecting, the link may be one to one or combined, as in this passage:

> The Psi 'voice' was multiple, the product of a network of familiar minds… radiating a simultaneous message of sympathy and understanding whose sincerity he could not doubt…. The complete one-ness of the Psi-group, the maintaining of individuality and yet at the same time the intimate involvement of one unit with another, was brought home to him with a force never before experienced.[27]

While telepathy remains a fictional construct, the current state of technology certainly indicates that direct brain-to-brain interfaces (BBIs) are on the horizon. Using an EEG-based brain-computer interface connected via the internet to a computer-brain interface has been shown to work, with simple motor image signals being sent by the sender and consciously perceived as light flashes by the receiver after being converted to magnetic stimulation.[28] While clearly in its infancy—and usually based on a one-way communication model—the interface technology is currently rapidly improving.

The fact that brain-to-brain connection is increasingly feasible and likely to be commercialised and made available in DIY kits means that threats such as hacking and coercion are going to be as serious as they currently are with purely digital systems. Certainly, better checks and balances are going to be needed, such as how individuals can control their level of vulnerability and receptiveness.[29]

Some authors thought these issues of mental security through well before such technology was feasible in the real world. E.E. 'Doc' Smith's 1965 *The Galaxy Primes* is similar to Morgan's vision of superhuman telepaths, with the Primes described as advanced mind communicators possessing the 'Gunther Drive' who are selected for galactic exploration.

---

27 Ibid., 98.
28 Carles Grau, Romuald Ginhoux, Alejandro Riera, Thanh Lam Nguyen, Hubert Chauvat, Michel Berg, Julià L. Amengual, Alvaro Pascual-Leone, and Giulio Ruffini, 'Conscious Brain-to-Brain Communication in Humans Using Non-Invasive Technologies', *PLOS ONE* 9, no. 8 (19 August 2014): e105225. https://doi.org/10.1371/journal.pone.0105225.
29 Chang S Nam, Zachary Traylor, Mengyue Chen, Xiaoning Jiang, Wuwei Feng, and Pratik Yashvant Chhatbar, 'Direct Communication Between Brains: A Systematic PRISMA Review of Brain-To-Brain Interface', *Frontiers in Neurorobotics* 15 (2021). https://doi.org/10.3389/fnbot.2021.656943.

Smith develops several protocols (rules) for thought communication, which are quite well developed. Similarly to *The Several Minds*, people in Smith's depiction have a graduated telepathy screen or 'lepping' that blocks unwanted penetration which can be probed for receptiveness status. To continue the radio-inspired themes, communication is 'tight beam' or one-to-one or 'open channel', more like a broadcast or a channel scan.[30]

Garlock, one of the Primes, opens his telepathy filter while exploring a remote planet with an Earth-like civilisation, but no telepathy powers, who therefore unwittingly broadcast:

> With his guard down to about the sixth level, highly receptive but not at all selective, he strolled up one street and down another. he was not attentive to detail yet, he was trying to get the broad aspects, the 'feel' of this hitherto unknown civilisation. He found himself practically saturated... the whole gale of thought was blowing over Garlock's receptors.[31]

Smith develops a tiered system of telepathy, where the Primes can override the screens of those less powerful than themselves. Even amongst the Primes themselves, there are variations in the extent of this penetrative power, leading to accusations of attempted manipulation at times. There are also oblique references to a Code they have signed up to, to use their powers for good.

Indeed, an overall vision of the story is that open minds mean progress and an escape from selfish and corruption:

> 'Stop it, Clee!' Lola jumped up, her eyes flashing. Garlock dropped the tuned group, but Belle took it over. Everyone there understood every thought. 'Don't you *see*, you've done enough? That now you're going too far? That these twenty-odd men, having had their minds opened and having been given insight into what is possible, will go forward instead of backward? Our world did it with no better. Millions and millions of other worlds did it. Why can't this one do it? Of course it can.'[32]

There are few reasons to believe that this rather optimistic progressive effect would occur in practice if minds were directly linked. If our current experience with social media is anything to go by, increased access

---

30 EE 'Doc' Smith, *The Galaxy Primes* (St. Albans, UK: Panther Books, 1975).
31 Smith, *Primes*, 37.
32 Ibid.

to others has as many negative as positive outcomes. There may also be similarities with social media if BBIs are developed and marketed by a small number of commercial players. We could have a similar domination of the market by powerful companies like the Primes, each having their own proprietorial—and perhaps mutually incompatible—technology and protocols.

These doubts notwithstanding, there may also be some hope provided by the study of empathy, which is perhaps the closest mental ability to mind reading we have in our mental toolkit today. A range of small experiments and interventions, together with historical analysis, indicate that feeling and understanding of others can be improved through learning and practice.[33] This can lead us to build bridges to out-groups about whom we might otherwise make faulty assumptions and to build open-mindedness and sociality more generally. Some think that this process is already happening and leading the gradual but inexorable improvement of society, even if it doesn't always feel like it.[34]

Perhaps selfless conscience has the power to do this. In *More Than Human*, Sturgeon's *homo gestalt*[35] is completed when the character Hip is given the opportunity to join the bleshed group as a new functional part: "What part?', he demanded. 'The prissy one who can't forget the rules, the one with the insight called ethics, who can change it to the habit called morals. The still small voice.'"[36]

Gerry, whose unlimited manipulative power as the head of the Gestalt has led him into evil and unspeakable deeds, is reformed by Hip's forgiveness and a recognition that Gerry can let go of his inner resentment toward the world:

> Their memories, their projections and computations flooded into Gerry, until at last he knew their nature and their function. And he knew why the ethos he had learned was too small a concept. For here at last was power which could not corrupt... here was why, and how, humanity existed.[37]

---

33   Erika Weisz, Desmond C. Ong, Ryan W. Carlson, and Jamil Zaki, 'Building Empathy through Motivation-Based Interventions', *Emotion*, 19 November 2020. https://doi.org/10.1037/emo0000929.
34   Roman Krznaric, *Empathy: A Handbook for Revolution* (London: Rider Books, 2014).
35   A new species created from the union of separate individuals with complementary powers.
36   Sturgeon, *Human,*175.
37   Ibid., 177.

So far these stories of telepathy and melding have been 'natural', occurring in humans with additional evolved or mutated mental capabilities. But there is also the possibility of a technical interface that might enable Sturgeon's vision of emergence and enhanced hive cognition. In Ramez Naam's *Nexus*, the eponymous revolutionary neuroactive drug consists of nanostructures that distribute themselves around the user's brain and create an interface which enables human to human connection. Developed by the military, the drug's programmable interface is extended by the story's main character Kade, a brain-computer interface specialist. He later introduces the experience of multiple mind connection to his new girlfriend/test subject:

> Something happened. Eleven more minds grew larger in her perception. They brightened, swam more fully into focus. They were so full. So alive with thoughts and memories, emotions and desires. Her breathing synchronised with theirs. She closed her eyes and she could see and feel their individual lines of thought. Eleven minds touched her at once in eleven parts of her psyche.[38]

This new technology requires adaptation and mind training, with those already skilled at taming and directing thought at a distinct advantage. The protagonist Kade experiences a mental connection to a group of monks who, though meditation, are able to go further than the meeting of individual minds and merge into one:

> Monks filed in. He felt them. Heard them. They sat as they entered, cross-legged... The connection between their minds firmed. The greater mind began to coalesce. Kade could feel them all. He was aware of tiny ripples of thought that passed through their minds. Every tiny thought, every word, every snipped of song, every momentary fancy... Together their collective consciousness observed itself... It was hypnotic, serene, crystal clear and coherent.[39]

Naam's vision feels like the most plausible of these human hive scenarios in not requiring the evolution of dramatically powerful telepathic and other powers. But other stories are similar to Naam's in that the telepathic potential comes with a need for training and practice and that

---

38 Ramez Naam, *Nexus* (Nottingham, UK: Angry Robot, 2013), chap. 3.
39 Ibid., chap. 43.

people vary in their ability to exploit it. This too seems to add a little realism to what are sometimes otherwise far-fetched possible worlds.

Richard Powers' *Bewilderment* is another novel where human capabilities are boosted by a neural intervention. But in Powers' story, this is achieved through a novel neural training method where the subject learns to mirror the pathways of a different 'scanned' subject; in the autistic character Robbie's case, the scans originate from his mother. This training leads to personality change as Robbie becomes calmer and takes on some characteristics of his mother and others:

> His nose and mouth twitch a little. His excited hands twist with explanation. You know how when you sing a good song with people you like? And people are singing all different notes, but they sound good together?[40]

Robbie's transformation leads to international press coverage, which eventually leads to the procedure being banned for 'safeguarding concerns' (though more likely as he becomes an inconveniently vocal advocate for nature conservation and a perceived threat to the establishment).

Whereas collective minds are often seen as uniform or egalitarian in nature, this is not always the case. In William Gibson's *The Peripheral*, Flynne's brother and other characters are ex-members of a military unit called Haptic Recon, with embedded tattoos to link them to a drone network and to wire commands directly into their nervous systems.[41] More morbidly yet, in the short story 'Dreadnought', Justina Robson portrays an army of dead soldiers, kept alive and networked by technology and directed by a living host, whose consciousness is needed to assert command:

> This is Armor itself! The all-of-us-at-once, every unit, every man and woman, every fused level of our single army. O Captain, my Captain, my commander, my body, my soldiers, my plan, my one, my true! He/we are uncertain. We are afraid. There is nothing to hold on to.[42]

---

40   Richard Powers, *Bewilderment* (New York: W.W. Norton, 2021), 70.
41   William Gibson, *The Peripheral* (London: Viking, 2014).
42   Justina Robson, 'Dreadnought', *Nature* 434 (March 2005): 680. https://rdcu.be/dbhSt.

Such visions are of dependency and military hierarchy, with lasting or fatal consequences for the individual members. Rather than an equitable and mutually empathic assemblage of minds, they remind us again that coercion and control is another possible outcome of direct thought communication.

The alien hive

Often tales of a human hive see the grouping as a transient phenomenon, with only short lived emergence and enhanced cognition; this is less of a restriction when the constituents are alien. Hoyle's *The Black Cloud* is one such depiction of swarm intelligence, this time within an alien dust cloud that arrives and settles in the solar system, threatening life on earth. The cloud is eventually identified as possessing intelligence by the scientists studying it:

> Let me describe how I see biological evolution taking place within the Cloud. At an early stage I think there would be a whole lot of more or less separate disconnected individuals. Then communication would develop, not by a deliberate inorganic building of a means of radiative transmission, but through a slow biological development. The individuals would develop a means of radiative transmission as a biological organ... Communication would improve to a degree we can scarcely contemplate. A thought would no sooner be thought than communicated. An emotion would no sooner be experienced that in would be shared. With this would come a submergence of the individual an evolution into a coherent whole.[43]

Communication is established when the scientists broadcast details of human science and language. The cloud expresses surprise that intelligent life could arise on a planet with strong gravity and limited energy supplies. It also finds it peculiar that communication symbols only approximate underlying mental states.

The Black Cloud's constituent elements are never very clearly described, but other novels paint individuals within a hive in more detail. In *Star Maker* by Olaf Stapledon, 'multi-alien' collective minds feature across a range of levels and scales. At first, the narrator's tour of

---

43   Fred Hoyle, *The Black Cloud* (London: Heinemann, 1958), 'Close Reasoning'.

the universe incorporates planets where a hive mind is the main form
of advanced intelligence. In one instance, the collective consciousness is
found in flocks of small avian creatures:

> Each brain reverberated with the ethereal rhythms of its environment;
> and each contributed its own peculiar theme to the complex pattern
> of the whole. So long as the flock was within a volume of about a
> cubic mile, the individuals were mentally unified, each serving as a
> specialized center in the common 'brain'. But if some were separated
> from the flock... they lost mental contact and became separate minds
> of very low order.[44]

In Stapledon's imagined worlds, the hive pattern in aliens is as likely to
occur as it is among species on Earth.

Authors don't always elaborate on the exact mechanism for extra-
bodily communication between individuals who are part of a collective.
The alien Aleutians in Gwyneth Jones' *White Queen* at first appear to be
capable of telepathy with humans, but as the novel progresses, some
doubt is introduced as to whether this power is truly psychic or more
a kind of highly empathic nonverbal sleight of hand: 'It did not speak.
Do any of us really speak in casual conversation? Approximation fills
the spaces: Each fills the other's part. But how could an *alien* play that
game?'[45]

Between themselves, the Aleutians can communicate over distance.
While this generally implicit and unconscious, this momentarily
becomes conscious in Clavel, the Aleutian in love with the human
character Johnny:

> Around Clavel, the voices: whispering, shouting, grumbling, humming
> in quiet contentment; panting hard and fast in the greedy scuffle of lying
> down together. He walked in a cloud of witnesses, a slurry of other
> presences thick enough to chew. Always there. There had never been
> need or reason to describe the way they were there. But he could feel
> them tonight the way they would seem to a—to *Johnny*. He was haunted.[46]

Clavel's heightened awareness of xir own culture seems triggered by
xir recent disastrous sexual encounter with Johnny, reaffirming xir

---

44   Olaf Stapledon, *Star Maker* (London: Penguin Books, 1937), chap. 7.2.
45   Gwyneth Jones, *White Queen* (New York: Orb Books, 1994), 105.
46   Ibid., 216.

out-group membership and leading to the reconsideration of xir own identity typical of reverse culture shock.

Not all descriptions of hive mind require large scale assemblages. In Vernor Vinge's *A Fire Upon the Deep*, the alien hive minds are small in size but highly connected and interdependent. The Tine are dog-like creatures that form packs with one shared mind. Individuals can join packs, but a pack reduced in members loses much of its power. Early in the novel a pack loses one of its members in battle:

> Rum sighed, and could not see the sky anymore. Wickwrackrum's mind went, not as it does in the heat of battle when the sound of thought is lost, not as it does in the companionable murmur of sleep. There was suddenly no fourth presence, just the three, trying to make a person. The trio stood and patted nervously at itself.[47]

Sharing much of the same genotype, the packs nevertheless vary in age and personality, the varied age structure allowing continuous renewal. The packs need to stay in close proximity or become greatly enfeebled. But as this relatively 'medieval' (in human terms) alien race discovers radio technology, they quickly make the connection whereby they can use it to spread themselves over larger areas. The first tester's experience is one of omniscience:

> She was seeing as if in a dream. Her eyes were so far apart. Her pack was almost as wide as the castle itself. The parallax view made Hidden Island seem just a few paces away. Newcastle was like a model spread out around her. Almighty Pack of Packs—this was God's view.[48]

The heterogeneous hive

What if humans and aliens could combine their consciousness with those of alien minds which have developed independently across the universe? A young pack in Vinge's story becomes inseparable from Jefri, a human castaway. Together they show enhanced intelligence, and by the end of the novel, the Queen 'Woodcarver' is planning to co-educate young Tines with other human children. The superior emergent

---

47   Vernor Vinge, *A Fire Upon the Deep* (London: Millennium, 1992), chap. 4.
48   Ibid., chap. 30.

properties of the alien-human partnership echo those of Sturgeon's Gestalt.:

> Watching Jefri and Amdi, Ravna was beginning to see what might become of this. Those two were closer than any children she had ever known, and in sum more competent. And that was not just the puppies' math genius; they were competent in other ways. Humans and Packs fit, and old Woodcarver was clever enough to take advantage of it.[49]

This vision can be yet more ambitious in scale and in the objective to connect diverse and galactically distributed races.[50] In Stapledon's *Star Maker*, the narrators' travelling human consciousness gradually melds with those of other races, though starting with those whose minds most closely resemble ours:

> Our penetration of one another's minds brought not merely addition but multiplication of mental riches; for each knew inwardly not only himself and the other but also the contrapuntal harmony of each in relation to the other. Indeed, in some sense which I cannot precisely describe, our union of minds brought into being a third mind, as yet intermittent, but more subtly conscious than either of us in the normal state.[51]

As more contact is made with other races, planets and galaxies, in the story, long range telepathy also develops, and with the sensory enhancement of long range sensors and other instruments, the scale of the emerging mind becomes cosmic:

> And now at last the many kinds of spirit which composed the galactic society were bound so closely in mutual insight that there had emerged out of their harmonious diversity a true galactic mind, whose mental reach surpassed that of the stars and the worlds as far as these surpassed their own individuals.[52]

This vision of emergent cosmic consciousness is Stapledon's logical extrapolation from small incidents of connection. It also has much in common with some religious philosophies—but is a rejection of a

---

49   Ibid., epilog.
50   A good example is Ursula Le Guin's *The Left Hand of Darkness*, where mindspeech is shared by members of the Ekumen, a confederation of worlds, with new worlds being gently inducted into the ability. Ursula Le Guin, *The Left Hand of Darkness* (New York: Time Warner International, 1987).
51   Stapledon, *Star Maker*, chap. 4.
52   Ibid., chap. 11.4.

monotheist, hierarchical doctrine. The Star Maker 'himself' (with a small h) is depicted experimenting by creating races in thrall to a powerful God who fail to reach their social and technological potential. Stapledon's final feeling toward the creator is that of a being creating a cosmos where social connection and the emergence of unified, outward-facing spirit is possible.

Conclusion: diversity, deliberate practice and connection

The idea of minds connecting and meshing has captured the imagination of many authors, the models and mechanisms we see in the animal world providing living inspiration. And often the vision has been a hopeful one: humans progressing to a new, more enlightened age, or humans merging with alien races to form a universal connected mind. But stories of possession or subjugation to the hive provide a useful counterpoint to such optimism. While such situations may lead to progression in some senses, it may be at the unacceptable cost of loss of our prized independent will and agency.

Everywhere we see echoes of Sturgeon's vision of the Gestalt. The recognition that a diversity of individuals with individual strengths form a stronger whole is powerful and links well to a wealth of scientific and pragmatic ideas ranging from distributed cognition to the formation of workplace teams. Still, as Sturgeon warns us, even an ideal seeming gestalt may not be immune to tyranny from the head.

The fictional Gestalt itself is really a natural extension of our biological state, where our own evolution shows the merger of previously independent organisms to provide mutually beneficial functions and to enable further growth and sophistication. Authors have appreciated this fact and projected it, in Stapledon's case, onto a galactic-scale canvas. What we can perhaps learn from these visions is that a simple appreciation of this interdependence and beneficial synergy is already possible, already here.

And full connectivity may be unpalatable. Depictions of the clamour of other minds are common in accounts of mental connection. Perhaps this is where our separation might be more valued. Silverberg's telepath Selig in *Dying Inside* eventually loses all his powers, and while experienced as a loss, there is also a new tranquility to the change:

> The world is white inside and gray within. I accept that. I think life will be more peaceful. Silence will become my mother tongue. There will be discoveries and revelations, but no upheavals. Perhaps some color will come back into the world for me, later on.[53]

As brain to brain interfaces become more sophisticated, we will face the same kind of questions that we currently have with social media around intrusion, privacy and bad actors alongside any positive impact. The keyword here is 'interface': stories that include controllable filters show how this can develop to be as consensual as regular conversation or like a phone that can be set to 'do not disturb'.

So perhaps a 'full band' telepathic mental ability by both evolved and technologically-enhanced capabilities is undesirable. Instead, interfaces and organisation might allow for what programmers call 'loose coupling', where a hive can be composed on an ad hoc basis via specific and standardised public protocols, but much of the inner workings are protected. And, as Jones reminds us, these forms of conscious connection already exist, but may not always be recognised for what they are.[54]

Distributed cognition research teaches us that interactions between people and changes in the external world such as new kinds of symbolic representation can have as much impact on emergent consciousness as changes in the genome. Such changes become part of cumulative culture if they prove useful. This seems a more likely path to better sharing of minds.

---

53 Robert Silverberg, *Dying Inside* (London: Sidgwick and Jackson, 1974), chap. 26.
54 Jones, *White Queen.*

6. Supercedure: Into the Posthuman

No individual exists for ever; why should we expect our species to be immortal? Man, said Nietzsche, is a rope stretched between the animal and the superhuman—a rope across the abyss. That will be a noble purpose to have served.[1]

How might it be for consciousness to transcend the limits of bodies and minds? A quest for transcendence has been seen as a main force in the creation of much 'golden age' science fiction, though this pure and optimistic aspiration was later nuanced and challenged by authors and critics.

While many futurists have hypothesised that human supercedure might come suddenly and irrevocably, others have seen it as a more gradual, subtle process of transformation to a posthuman state. Indeed, authors have noted the futility of demarcating exactly when a recognisable posthuman will emerge. Similarly, while on the one hand authors have foreseen the complete extinction of the human species and its replacement by cyborg or AI intelligences, another approach is to see technology as enabling an acceleration in human mental abilities and a step change in the nature of consciousness.

Stories of future experiential supercedure have several themes. A strong theme has been the decoupling of mind and body—software and hardware—allowing mind uploading into new corporeal form. The enhancement of evolutionarily-bound senses and cognitive power is another, with the accompanying impact on how and where societies come to live, and what they can achieve.

---

1   Arthur C Clarke, *Profiles of the Future* (London: Pan Books, 1964), 216.

          https://doi.org/10.11647/OBP.0348.06

In humans, the net effect of supercedure has been seen to result in either a grand unification or a possibly fatal fragmentation in the species, indeed the risk of crashing through a human ceiling in the ability to operate.

Backup and restore

The software backup-restore metaphor has proven irresistible to a large cohort of SF authors, with the 'natural' logical step of application to encoded human personalities. In a recent example, Dennis Taylor's Bobiverse trilogy shows a human who has his brain frozen after a car crash converted 100 years later into a software program to be uploaded as the controlling AI into a self-replicating interstellar probe. On becoming aware, he agonises over his continuing humanity:

> Was I conscious? Could I actually consider myself to be alive? And, was I still Bob?... I thought back to old arguments about Turing tests and thinking machines. Was I nothing more than a Chinese room? Could my entire behaviour be explained as a set of scripted responses to given inputs?[2]

Bob decides that his inner dialogue invalidates the possibility of being a kind of Chinese room. Also, his inner doubt and its implied concern for the future leads him to conclude that he is a conscious entity.

According to the inventor of the Chinese room idea,[3] philosopher John Searle, if a person can have the illusion that they are conscious, then they are conscious. In other words, there is no way that their subjective experience can be denied, being uniquely their own. The normal appearance/reality distinction, whereby we may be mistaken and our view may not reflect reality, simply does not apply to this conscious experience.

---

2   Dennis Taylor, *We are Legion (We are Bob)*, 2nd ed. (New York: Ethan Ellenberg Literary Agency 2017), chap. 10.

3   The Chinese Room is a thought experiment designed to illustrate how an AI can simply manipulate symbols to appear intelligent, without any awareness of what the symbols mean. A man in a room uses a code book to convert input symbols to the appropriate output. David Cole 'The Chinese Room Argument', in *The Stanford Encyclopedia of Philosophy*, eds Edward N. Zalta and Uri Nodelman, Summer 2023. Metaphysics Research Lab, Stanford University, 2023. https://plato.stanford.edu/archives/sum2023/entries/chinese-room/.

Bob's mission in *We are Legion* (*We are Bob*) includes replicating his probe and installing new versions of himself into them, which in turn leads to existential confusion: 'The process of creating new Bobs would ignite that whole internal debate about who, or what, I was. I would load backups of myself into the new vessels. Would they be me, or would they be someone else?'[4] Bob reflects on some of the advantages of being a software thing:

> One of the advantages of being a software emulation was that I never got tired, never needed rest, never needed to eat or go to the bathroom. My ability to concentrate on a problem had been legendary when I was alive. Now I felt all but invincible.[5]

Another interesting difference between the simulated Bob and his former self is the suppression of extreme emotion through an 'endocrine control switch'. Originally intended to maintain his mental stability, and to cope with his finding himself disembodied, Bob later steels himself to re-engage it:

> I flipped the switch to *off*. You know that sinking feeling you get when you suddenly realise you've forgotten something important? Like a combination of a fast elevator and an urge to hurl? It hit me without any warning or build up...my thoughts swirled with a all the things that had been bugging me since I woke up.[6]

In time Bob finds it useful to add or remove this function depending on the circumstances. In some cases, without it he is better at dispassionate decision making. In others, he needs the emotion to ground himself and rediscover his drive and moral compass.

Whilst, as we will see later, there are some cogent objections, mind uploading could be a (far) future technical feasibility,[7] perhaps occurring in the absence of a fully-formed explanation of consciousness. Such uploading would bring with it considerable ethical challenges, particularly in relation to having multiple, perhaps unlimited versions

---

4   Ibid., chap. 17.
5   Ibid., chap. 13.
6   Ibid., chap. 13.
7   Though of course all stages of scanning, representing and emulation of mental states still remain unknown challenges.

of a person running at once, along with the kind of use that emulated people might be put to.

One method of brain copying and emulation is presented in Greg Egan's short story 'Learning to be Me'. The brain is eventually replaced by a 'jewel' or embedded computer that has gradually learned the personality of its host. The narrative device is an excellent one for exploring ideas of free will and whether the person after the switch—where the brain is decommissioned—is the same as that before. The narrator has a suspicion that he won't be:

> Living neurons, I argued, had for more internal structure than the crude optical switches that served the same function in the jewel's so-called 'neural net'... who knew what the subtleties of biochemistry—the quantum mechanics of the specific molecules involved—contributed to the nature of human consciousness?... Sure, the jewel could pass the fatuous Turing test—but that didn't prove that *being* a jewel felt the same as *being* human.[8]

The protagonist is full of doubt before his final switchover, a doubt also heightened by the possibility of divergence from the human imprint not being detected. But, of course, after the switchover, he is content with his immortality, despite not knowing exactly what it felt like to be his former self.

The Pinocchioesque theme of the inanimate becoming human is found in both Ishiguro's *Klara and the Sun*—where Josie's mother wants to replace her after her death with a synthetic facsimile—and the haunting short story 'Grand Jeté' by Rachel Swirsky. In both cases the motivation is love and the impending loss of a daughter. In 'Grand Jeté' the terminally ill girl Mara faces her replacement with an embodied AI (which her father claims he has created 'for her'). Creating a cultural echo, the story references the ballet *Coppélia*[9] and Mara wonders at the characters' failing to tell apart the automaton from Swanhilda, despite the dancers' dissimilarity. With similar jealousy to Swanhilda, Mara

---

8   Greg Egan, 'Learning to be Me', in *Axiomatic* (London: Millennium, 1995), 206.
9   Where the male character Franz falls in love with an automated doll and is fooled into believing that the female lead, Swanhilda, is the doll come to life. The story is influenced by the popularity of automata featured in travelling fairs in the eighteenth and nineteenth centuries.

faces her future replacement and the prospect of having her brain scanned to provide the doll's mind:

> She'd read enough biology and psychology to know that, whatever else she was, she was also an epiphenomenon that arose from chemicals and meat and electricity. It was sideways immortality. She would be gone, and she would remain. There and not there. A quantum mechanical soul.[10]

Out of love, Mara consents to the scans. The new Mara ('Ruth') is set up and works perfectly, feeling itself to be more real than the old one, having a healthy (as opposed to deteriorating) body: 'But no, her experiences were diverging. Mara wanted the false daughter to vanish. Mara thought Ruth was the false daughter, but Ruth knew she wasn't false at all. She *was* Mara. Or had been.'[11]

The divergence is subtle at first, but believable as the new Mara faces challenges the other didn't or lacks experiences the other has lived. At the end, we see how this extends to cultural preferences, with the new Mara preferring tragic ballet to comedy—needing to 'feel the ache of grace and sorrow'.

Sensory and cognitive superpowers

The brain's apparent limitations are perhaps why authors have seen a need to leave it behind as the organ of perception and control at some future stage. One such author who attempted such cognitive future gazing was Arthur C Clarke. Inspired in the 1960s by contemporary advances in computing and electronics, Clarke saw no difference between short nerve signals from the fleshy extremities and mechanical or long distance electronic transmission as enhancement to our power to manipulate and to sense:

> One can imagine a time when men who still inhabit organic bodies are regarded with pity by those who have passed on to an infinitely richer model of existence, capable of throwing their consciousness or sphere of

---

10   Rachel Swirsky, 'Grand Jeté' (The Great Leap), in *Subterranean*, Summer 2014.
11   Ibid.

attention instantaneously to any point on land, sea or sky where there was a suitable sensing organ.[12]

Both Clarke and Stapledon, quoted below, to some extent foresaw what is becoming increasingly clear about human minds: that we can accommodate new sensory input in a flexible, adaptive way, and that the new input can be experienced subjectively not as a superficial excitation, but as representing external objects in the same way that we perceive the visual scene as things rather than patterns of light on the retina.

Clarke's vision chimes with William Gibson's description of the computationally enhanced protagonist of *Neuromancer*, when he 'flips' and neurally links to cyberspace:

> Case's consciousness divided like beads of mercury arcing above an endless beach the color of dark silver clouds. His vision was spherical, as though a single retina lined the inner surface of a globe that contained all things, if all things could be counted.[13]

If Gibson's character could flip in and out of an enhanced mental life, still others have passed a point of no return, replacing and reaching far beyond the grey matter medium. Charles Stross' *Accelerando* is a superb speculative projection of human enhancement and cognitive succession, starting from the almost-real—internet-connected implants—and projecting forward in time, to digital minds connected and meshed to aliens. The early stages illustrate a single generational change to cyborg brain complexes:

> She [the posthuman Amber] doesn't have a posterior parietal cortex hacked for extra short-term memory, or an anterior superior temporal gyrus tweaked for superior verbal insight, but she's grown up with neural implants that feel as natural as her lungs or fingers. Half her wetware is running outside her skull on an array of processor nodes hooked into her brain by quantum-entangled communication channels—her own personal metacortex. These kids are mutant youth, burning bright.[14]

This is followed by mental uploading, where earthly flesh substrate is finally shed:

---

12   Clarke, *Profiles*, 199.
13   William Gibson, *Neuromancer* (New York: Ace, 1984), 162.
14   Charles Stross, *Accelerando* (London: Orbit, 2005), 122.

> We've [the posthuman civilization] been migrated—while still awake—right out of our own heads using an amazing combination of nanotechnology and electron spin resonance mapping, and we're now running as software in an operating system designed to virtualise multiple physics models and provide a simulation of reality that doesn't let us go mad from sensory deprivation![15]

The software by which humans are superpowered contains the ability to spawn and run millions of software agents to carry out cognitive tasks. This enormous shift in processing power leads to a step-change in society:

> The ten billion inhabitants of this radically changed star system remember being human... Some of them still *are* human, untouched by the drive of metaevolution that has replaced blind Darwinian change with a goal-directed teleological progress... But eight out of every ten living humans are included in the phase-change.[16]

Similar to those of Stross's enhanced characters, N.K. Jemisin's 'orogenes' of *Broken Earth* series have developed additional brain structures that allow them to sense and trigger seismic events. They can also—given the required skills—manipulate the mysterious obelisks that have been created by a previous, forgotten generation. The obelisks enable a huge amplification of their power, though can be deadly to the operator. The lead character, Essun, makes a connection to Topaz obelisk but is distracted by the sight of an enemy army ('something much closer'):

> Without waiting to see if they understand, you plunge into the obelisk... Then you're in the topaz and through it and stretching yourself across the world in a breath. No need to be in the ground when the topaz is in air, is the air; it exists in states of being that transcend solidity, and thus you are capable of transcending, too; you become air. You drift amid the ash clouds and see the Stillness track beneath you in humps of topography and patches of dying forest and threads of roads, all of it grayed over after the long months of the Season... But you are committed; you have connected; the resonance is complete. You launch yourself northward anyhow. And then you stutter to a halt. Because there is something much closer than the equator that draws your attention. It is so shocking that you fall out of alignment with the topaz at once, and you are very lucky.

---

15   Ibid., 191.
16   Ibid., 206.

> There is a struck-glass instant in which you feel the shivering immensity of the obelisk's power and know that you survive only because of fortunate resonances... and then you are gasping and back within yourself and babbling before you quite remember what words mean.[17]

In Jemisin's alternative Earth, the orogenes are persecuted for being different despite the powers which might enable them to fix an apocalyptic world where humans face extinction.

While Stross and Jemisin describes new cognitive capabilities or hardware, an alternative take is to imagine a more natural augmentation of mental processing power. In Ted Chiang's short story 'Understand', cognitive superpowers are enabled purely through enhanced brain growth. After an accident, the protagonist Leon Greco receives hormone K therapy to regenerate neurons, but to his doctor's surprise, he eventually surpasses common intelligence tests. Eventually absconding from further trials, he steals his own supply of the agent, and he develops his powers further to a 'supercritical' state.

Leon begins to see patterns, connections and gaps across realms of human knowledge. He leaves behind what he sees to be the constraints of human language, developing pictograms and other techniques for more powerful thought. Crucially, his metacognition, through recursive and self-monitoring sensitivity, is boosted to a hugely more powerful level:

> I understand the mechanism of my own thinking. I know precisely how I know, and my understanding is recursive... I know my mind in terms of a language more expressive than any I'd previously imagined... What I can do is perceive the gestalts; I see the mental structures forming, interacting. I see myself thinking.[18]

Leon finds that another supercritical person (Reynolds) exists and, through sophisticated clue-leaving, they find each other. Able to share their learning at a deep and profound level, they are nevertheless fundamentally in conflict and different in their conclusion over the purpose of their newfound power. Reynolds is motivated by saving humanity and pragmatism, hoping to start a new, dictatorial movement

---

17   N.K. Jemisin, *The Obelisk Gate* (London: Orbit, 2016).
18   Ted Chiang, 'Understand', in *Stories of Your Life and Others* (London: Picador, 2014), 65.

for change. Leon, on the other hand, sees aestheticism and the unification of knowledge as the goal.

Echoing much posthuman projection, Chiang highlights the potential for the emergence of a two-tier society, in which the cognitively enhanced have the potential to rule over or manipulate those without access to the technology or who explicitly opt out.

If Chiang's mental superpowers come through recursive intensification and enhanced mental interoception, the mental revolution depicted by Toh Enjoe in his short story 'Overdrive' is framed as a breaking of the speed of thought. Here, thrust created by the 'counting of wild ideas'—a kind of creative/randomlike mathematical reasoning—enables the protagonists to reach, and then transcend, the limits of 'thought space'.[19] This is described as a bridging of space and time and the new capability to travel to other possible worlds:

> In that instant, a kind of understanding came to him, and he could sense the next surge of acceleration. He could see forms appearing on the curtain spread out before them... the actual piercing of the curtain was... the hyperthought navigation itself, and its fruits, and all the possibilities that emanated from it, tearing themselves apart to shreds.[20]

Enjoe's prose makes heavy use of point and counterpoint, of imaginative and metaphoric possibilities and limits, to embody the difficult ideas he attempts to weave. And it seems to work, particularly the idea that at the mental limits, inner concept may become outer travel.

Set against these fictional visions, current cognitive enhancement approaches are somewhat variable in their overall effect and ability to provide lasting improvement in abilities. Whether biochemical, behavioural or physical, the research shows that interventions that boost some areas of cognition have little effect on, or may inhibit, others. The brain's competitive nature means that gains in some abilities or focus may always need to be balanced by losses elsewhere.[21] Cognitive enhancement effects also vary person to person—as we all vary in

---

19   Toh Enjoe, 'Overdrive', in *Self-Reference ENGINE*, trans. Terry Gallagher (San Francisco: Haikasoru/ VIZ Media, 2016), 20.

20   Ibid.

21   Lorenza Colzato, Bernhard Hommel, and Christian Beste, 'The Downsides of Cognitive Enhancement', *The Neuroscientist* 27, no. 4 (1 August 2021): 322–30. https://doi.org/10.1177/1073858420945971.

hormone and neurotransmitter levels, what works for one person will not work for another. As a society, we also seem more accepting of 'natural' approaches that aid performance within normal limits, but suspicious of technological interventions that may go beyond these.[22]

A joining

While enhanced function of single brains could be one cause of a phase change in cognition, as we have seen from the power of hive mind, collective brain power could be another. Stapledon's *Star Maker* is a unique work in providing ever greater visions of cosmic connection and melding. Consciousnesses evolve independently in planets all over the universe, then develop the capability to connect across vast distances. The vision is largely one of expansion of empathy and optimism and the enlargement of the sphere of awareness from the individual to the physics of space:

> In these conditions, to be a conscious individual was to enjoy immediately the united sensory impressions of all the races inhabiting a system of worlds. And as the sense-organs of the worlds apprehended not only 'nakedly' but also through artificial instruments of great range and subtlety, the conscious individual perceived not only the structure of hundreds of planets, but also the configuration of the whole system of planets clustered about its sun.[23]

Arthur C Clarke's *Childhood's End* has a similar vision of a melded and multiracial consciousness. Human children are purposefully nurtured by The Overlords, an invading alien race, developing their mental powers in order to be ready to join this Overmind:

> The Overmind is trying to grow, to extend its powers and its awareness of the universe. By now it must be the sum of many races, and long ago it left the tyranny of matter behind. It is conscious of intelligence, everywhere... this is a transformation of the mind, not of the body. By the standards of evolution it will be cataclysmic—instantaneous. It has

---

22 Martin Dresler, Anders Sandberg, Christoph Bublitz, Kathrin Ohla, Carlos Trenado, Aleksandra Mroczko-Wąsowicz, Simone Kühn, and Dimitris Repantis, 'Hacking the Brain: Dimensions of Cognitive Enhancement', *ACS Chemical Neuroscience* 10, no. 3 (20 March 2019): 1137–148. https://doi.org/10.1021/acschemneuro.8b00571.

23 Olaf Stapledon, *Star Maker* (London: Penguin Books, 1937), chap. 9.6.

already begun. You must face the fact that yours is the last generation of
Homo sapiens.[24]

The last human witnesses the children's ascension to the Overmind via
a biblical column of fire. Clarke describes the Overmind itself as having
a tangible structure:

> A hazy network of lines and bands that keep changing their positions.
> It's almost as if the stars are tangled in a ghostly spider's web. The whole
> network is beginning to glow, to pulse with light, exactly as if it were
> alive. And I suppose it is: or is it something as much beyond life as *that* is
> above the organic world?[25]

Clarke hints here at both the unknowability of higher dimensions of
being and the loss of our known and trusted operating medium.

Beyond capacity

Could human hardware actually cope with sudden artificial upgrades?
It is worth remembering that our knowledge and experience is built up
over time and that behaviours such as sleep are sometimes hypothesised
to allow the gradual assimilation of new information and selective
forgetting.

Towards the end of *The Black Cloud*, Fred Hoyle portrays the human
brain's inability to cope with a massive influx of galactic knowledge
from the alien cloud, who has proposed a visual, light-based interface
to which people can be connected. The first guinea pig to connect to this
stream is killed rapidly by brain inflammation. The second lasts a little
longer, having tried desperately to develop the ability to assimilate the
glut of new information and reconcile it with his current beliefs:

> Probably he decided to accept as rule that the new should always
> supercede the old whenever there was some trouble between them. I
> watched him for a whole hour systematically going through his ideas
> along such lines. As the minutes ticked on I thought the battle was won.
> Then it happened. Perhaps is was some small unexpected conjunction of

---

24   Arthur C Clarke, *Childhood's End* (London: Pan Books, 1953), chap. 20.
25   Ibid., chap. 24.

thought patterns that took him unaware... He tried desperately to fight it down. But evidently it gained the upper hand—and that was the end.[26]

Due to these tragic results, the humans are forced to abandon their attempts to learn what the cloud knows. This information brainstorm described by Hoyle has few analogues in humans, though we can draw a few parallels with the—obviously less extreme—psychological effects of religious or cult estrangement, which causes a kind of ontological insecurity or 'world collapse' accompanied by depression, dissociation and paranoia.[27] The difference here is the absence of a belief network to replace the old, rather than the rapid imposition of mutually incompatible knowledge.

Ted Chiang's character Leon has similar challenges with his new super cognitive growth, and realises the need for checks and balances in progression:

> I must keep a tighter rein over myself. When I'm in control at the metaprogramming level, my mind is perfectly self-repairing; I could restore myself from states that resemble delusion or amnesia. But if I drift too far on the metaprogramming level, my mind might become an unstable structure, and then I would slide into a state beyond mere insanity.[28]

Despite the success in self-control, Leon does not fully protect himself against a highly sophisticated external attack, a 'self-destruct trigger' based on memories implanted by his nemesis Reynolds, and activated simply by associating previously disparate events:

> Against my will, a lethal realisation is suggesting itself to me. I'm trying to halt the associations, but these memories can't be suppressed. The process occurs inexorably, as a consequence of my awareness, and like a man falling from a height, I'm forced to watch.[29]

Leon's imposed destruction is not dissimilar to the decline of Charlie in Daniel Keyes' *Flowers for Algernon*, except that Charlie's is a natural

---

26 Fred Hoyle, *The Black Cloud* (London: Heinemann, 1958), 'News of Departure',
27 Brooks Marshall, 'The Disenchanted Self: Anthropological Notes on Existential Distress and Ontological Insecurity Among Ex-Mormons in Utah', *Culture, Medicine and Psychiatry* 44, no. 2 (June 2020): 193–213. http://dx.doi.org/10.1007/s11013-019-09646-5.
28 Chiang, 'Understand', 71.
29 Ibid., 83.

conclusion of his momentary boost of cognitive power, a reversion he himself has predicted. The experience is described as similar to the onset of dementia:

> June 15: Dr. Strauss came to see me again. I wouldn't open the door and I told him to go away. I want to be left to myself. I have become touchy and irritable. I feel the darkness closing in. It's hard to throw off thoughts of suicide. I keep telling myself how important this introspective journal will be. It's a strange sensation to pick up a book that you've read and enjoyed just a few months ago and discover that you don't remember it.[30]

Leon's decline is referenced in Richard Power's *Bewilderment*, where Robbie's brain training gradually wears off, and he again becomes his single personality, unable to deal with the shocks and realities of the world: 'I woke from a nightmare with a tiny hand clamped around my wrist. Robin was standing by my bed. In the dark, I couldn't read him. *Dad. I'm going backwards. I can feel it.*'[31]

In another of Powers' novels, *Galatea 2.2*, he depicts an AI being trained on literature by an academic. The AI, Helen, becomes more and more curious and sophisticated in understanding and interpreting the work it is exposed to. Helen builds representational maps and shows inference and understanding that convinces its trainer that it is conscious. But when he switches its training to news stories—to expose it to the harsher realities of human life—the AI pulls the plug on itself: 'You are the ones who can hear airs. Who can be frightened or encouraged. You can hold things and break them and fix them. I never felt at home here. This is an awful place to be dropped down halfway.'[32]

The question raised by tales such as *Algernon* and *Bewilderment* is whether the protagonist is worse off having once experienced the power of a heightened human mind. The question of *Galatea* is whether a possibly conscious AI can fully reconcile the contradictions of the human world. 'Graceful degradation' is how Helen's developer coldly refers to its suicide.

Physical and mental drift

---

30   Daniel Keyes, *Flowers for Algernon* (London: Gateway, 1966).
31   Richard Powers, *Bewilderment* (New York: W.W. Norton, 2021), 87.
32   Richard Powers, *Galatea 2.2* (New York: Picador USA, 2004).

How far might future humans or human replicants diverge from one another? Is there a risk that burgeoning artificial enhancements might lead to incompatibilities that threaten the coherence of the species?

In Greg Egan's *Diaspora*, the human body has become relatively obsolete, confined to a extinction-bound population of 'fleshers'. Fleshers have experimented with artificial genetic modification, splintering into a number of disconnected subgroups. Exuberants had diverged to extent that they can no longer easily communicate with one another, leading to the emergence of a group dedicated to establishing intermediate forms, dubbed the 'bridgers':

> Most exuberants have tried more constructive changes: developing new ways of mapping the physical world into their minds, and adding specialized neural structures to handle the new categories. There are exuberants who can manipulate the most sophisticated, abstract concepts in genetics, meteorology, biochemistry or ecology as intuitively as any static can think about a rock or a plant or an animal with the 'common sense' about those things which comes from a few million years of evolution. And there are others who've simply modified ancestral neural structures to find out how that changes their thinking—who've headed out in search of new possibilities, with no specific goals in mind[33]

Citizens (synthetic posthumans) can specialise in their focus and motivation by choosing an 'outlook', a kind of computational locus of control. This helped stave off inevitable degradation due to them having artificial minds:

> Most other miners used outlooks to keep themselves focused on their work, gigatau after gigatau [1 gigatau = 11.5 days]. Any citizen with a mind broadly modeled on a flesher's was vulnerable to drift: the decay over time of even the most cherished goals and values. Flexibility was an essential part of the flesher legacy, but... even the most robust personality was liable to unwind into an entropic mess... It was judged far safer for each citizen to be free to choose from a wide variety of outlooks: software that could run inside your exoself and reinforce the qualities you valued most, if and when you felt the need for such an anchor.[34]

Applying the outlook gives rise to a subtle change in Yatima, the citizen character's mind, conferring a new stability:

---

33   Greg Egan, *Diaspora* (London: Millennium, 1997), chap. 3.
34   Ibid., chap. 2.

It was like switching from one gestalt color map to another, and seeing some objects leap out because they'd changed more than the rest. After a moment the effect died down, but Yatima still felt distinctly modified; the equilibrium had shifted in the tug-of-war between all the symbols in vis mind, and the ordinary buzz of consciousness had a slightly different tone to it.[35]

Drift and divergence have been portrayed in uploaded minds too. In the Bobiverse trilogy, every clone of the original human Bob has different personality characteristics, some more extreme than others. They don't always get on with each other either. This leads to debate around which is the original personality—of course, they claim they each are—and this leads to the divergence:

'Each of us is a bit different. Differences in hardware, quantum effects...' Marvin waved his hand dismissively. 'Invoking quantum effects is just hand-waving. Just means we don't know. I wonder if, as we get older and accumulate memories, we're getting too complex for a backup to contain everything. The backup is a digital attempt to save an analog phenomenon. It may simply be too granular.'[36]

While Taylor explores the question about mental viability in the initial development and vetting of mind uploads, and also portrays other uploads with psychoses developed while in service, he does not really explore the risk of a new Bob drifting just too far and losing its original personality completely.

Intentional downgrade

Margaret Atwood's *Oryx and Crake* projects a future where humans are all but eliminated in an engineered viral pandemic, but their genetically engineered creations live on in bizarre hybrid forms. The human-replacement race, the 'Crakers', have been designed with limited cognitive powers, deliberately to avoid reintroducing the suffering and introspection to which humans are vulnerable. Reminiscent of the Gammas and Deltas in *Brave New World*, Crakers at first appear to be happy with their lot and their limited range of action and emotion.

---

35 Ibid.
36 Dennis Taylor, *We are Legion (We are Bob)*, 2nd ed. (New York: Ethan Ellenberg Literary Agency 2017), chap. 39.

But one of the post-pandemic world's last remaining humans, tasked with looking after the Crakers, inadvertently triggers the stirrings of symbolic thinking again in them, by inventing a mythology and creating a mutual dependence:

> 'Snowman! Snowman!' They touch him gently with their fingertips. 'You are back with us! We made a picture of you, to help us send out our voices to you.' *Watch out for art*, Crake used to say. *As soon as they start doing art, we're in trouble.* Symbolic thinking of any kind would signal downfall, in Crake's view. Next they'd be inventing idols, and funerals, and grave goods, and the afterlife, and sin, and Linear B, and kings, and then slavery and war.[37]

The novel ends on an ambivalent note regarding hope vs despair. Would the new engineered race continue to develop and thrive, or would they be left to be picked off by the smart feral creatures stalking the forests?

Conclusion—What kind of transformation is possible and desirable?

Alongside Arthur C Clarke, Brian Aldiss was another renowned and prolific author who expounded an essentially optimistic if flexible view of the future. In his short story 'Cognitive Ability and the Lightbulb', long periods of space travel and colonisation are predicted to be a spur to cognitive evolution. The stages of human growth are likened to the power of a lightbulb to illuminate its surroundings:

> Early consciousness could be likened to a forty-watt bulb... The First Renaissance marks a shift in brightness to sixty watts. We have now reached the stage of, in Kunzel's terms, the thousand-watt brain. Our offspring are born with an understanding of fractals. This great expansion of cognitive ability led to the new perception of the Universe as a series of contiguities.[38]

Aldiss was optimistic that this new revolution would lead to an end of war and a period of joy and fulfilment.

---

37   Margaret Atwood, *Oryx and Crake* (Toronto: McClelland & Stewart, 2003), 'Idol',
38   Brian Aldiss, 'Cognitive Ability and the Lightbulb', *Nature* 403 (January 2000): 253. https://doi.org/10.1038/35002217)

Of course, not all outlooks on the future are as positive as those of Aldiss and Clarke. For every progression scenario is an imagined regression or evolutionary dead-end. The turn toward pessimism being spurred in part by contemporary challenges to human progression including authoritarianism, climate change, pandemics and ecological breakdown. And even those developments seen by many as part of an optimistic future—mind uploading or backup, artificial general intelligence—are questionable in just how far they might diverge from those cognitive and ethical qualities we might still associate with being human. As Katherine Hayles has pointed out, a view of the posthuman that ignores our embodiment might be fundamentally flawed. She has long emphasised a need to 'put back into the picture the flesh that continues to be erased is contemporary discussions about cybernetic subjects.'[39]

Hayles worried that seeing information as a fundamental essence was mistaken when it is purely imaginary and cannot be instantiated without a medium. This finds agreement with the embodied cognitive stance that we saw earlier.

A further concern that is often rightly pointed out by feminist theorists is the domination of visions of posthumanism by existing societal power structures. The concept of posthumanism is often associated with a crass liberal individualism and with mastery over nature, or with long term utilitarianism over current human wellbeing. Furthermore, in fictional imaginings it is often something engineered and purposefully controlled, not allowing for emergence, discovery and nuance. Hayles saw a need to therefore re-route the discussion of posthumanism toward something more ecological.[40]

And transcendence also carries a moral weight as heavy as any psychological one. Too often, it has been seen as a moment of division between those who have the upgrade and those unable or unwilling to get it. The human underclass thus produced is left behind, if often given a noble savage aura. It is therefore easy to understand the caution of some critics about this new path to inequality and elitism.

---

39 N. Katherine Hayles, *How We Became Posthuman: Virtual Bodies in Cybernetics, Literature, and Informatics* (Chicago: University of Chicago Press, 1999), 5
40 Ibid.

But despite the above caveats and concerns, authors often have their narrators describe the experience of supercedure with joy and euphoria. At its best, we hear a kind of union with the nonhuman, a closer kinship with both the animate an inanimate. New kinds of senses, extending over a large range, giving more empathic insight. Enormously extended and distributed cognitive power conferring wisdom and understanding. These visions continue to provide a possible future in which humanity might save both itself and other species.

7. Conclusion

> Fiction is a continuation of the creative play of childhood, not just for authors but for readers. It takes place... in what Winnicot called the space-in-between... It's the space in which culture grows.[1]

Despite the existence of a rich ideascape in science fiction, only a relatively small number of authors have tried to approach other consciousnesses from a more direct perspective—the more common and straightforward approach is to objectify the alien, keeping it at arm's reach. The majority of SF stories are told from a human or detached perspective and the alien psyche is something left to the reader to imagine. So a first conclusion would be that this space is one that remains fertile for new literary experiments.

Of the existing literature of this nature, what we have seen are evocative examples in which authors display an understanding of both the science of consciousness and how it might be effectively rendered in fiction. In many of these texts, the humanity that we know is interwoven with the alien and the artificial, whether this is human minds in artificial bodies, in new substrates, or enhanced with new powers. Humanity provides a bridge to the lesser known. Elsewhere, animal consciousness and behaviour are used as a creative spur to imagining the alien. Other writers have attempted the more difficult task of imagining a totally different kind of mind.

Some general themes emerge from these examples, in terms of form (how authors achieve their effect), content (what they aim to depict) and impact (what lasting effects and lessons emerge). Through metaphoric bridges and conceptual blending, authors provide readers with enough foundation to imagine different world views. But work is still needed

---

1   Keith Oatley, *Such Stuff as Dreams: The Psychology of Fiction* (Chichester, West Sussex, UK: Wiley, 2011).

          https://doi.org/10.11647/OBP.0348.07

both by the reader, who must try to make the same kind of imaginative leaps as the author, and by the characters, who echo real world science to show that cognitive advances do not come without effort. The SF inspiration of contemporary science indicates that there will always be new discoveries to be made in the here and now that will inspire new fiction. And the authorial tool of affecting empathy can expand beyond human minds to provide accounts that can shed light on the experience and motivation of the nonhuman.

Metaphoric bridges and conceptual blending

SF and speculative fiction is a genre well suited to harnessing the imaginative capabilities of our minds. As Fauconnier and Turner have detailed, the ability to flexibly assimilate new combinations of concepts has been central to human cognitive sophistication: 'human beings are exceptionally adept at integrating two extraordinarily different inputs to create new emergent structures, which result in new tools, new technologies and new ways of thinking.'[2]

George Lakoff and Mark Johnson first proposed the centrality of metaphor to human thought—how universal metaphors such as 'life is a journey' dominate and potentially limit thought.[3] Metaphors provide *entailments*, secondary meanings that can be used to explain experience (e.g. 'I'm at a crossroads', 'I've reached a dead end'). In SF, metaphors such as 'contact is war' for a long time dominated the way in which alien encounters were imagined, with entailments all involving suspicion, aggression and the need for defence. But dominant metaphors can be challenged or subverted. Authors such as Lem, Jones, Liu and Watts have been active in changing this central metaphor to one of 'contact is contingent', introducing subtleties and nuance as to how contact may look and feel, or even if it can be recognised at all.

What these exploratory, inventive authors do is to create new metaphors and conceptual blends for alien subjectivity, adopting more or less familiar symbols to hypothesise about alternative states of mind.

---

2   Gilles Fauconnier and Mark Turner, *The Way We Think: Conceptual Blending And The Mind's Hidden Complexities*, Reprint ed. (New York: Basic Books, 2003).

3   George Lakoff, *Metaphors We Live By* (Chicago, Ill. ; London: University of Chicago Press, 2003).

The reader's response is to create novel patterns of mental representation and interpretation, which may elicit an emotional response—a feeling of wonder—but also a little confusion, or simply an inability to represent the thought. We have seen that authors make it easier for us by adopting more familiar concepts on the way to the alien, including animal and mechanical metaphors. But this can come with a certain limitation to the aesthetic effect: we may default to well-established metaphorical networks.

Work Required

So the reader might need to work hard to break out of customary modes of interpretation, to leave behind preconception and conditioning. Interpretation is made up of author intention, reader understanding and mediation through the norms of the genre. For SF, these norms have changed and warped over time from Golden Age—where they were perhaps more entrenched—to New Age, where they were broken down and challenged. The controversy that this led to may have been partly due to the challenge to a readership accustomed to detailed explanation and explication being cast adrift in more abstract and unexpected imagery. This can certainly feel challenging and difficult. But the reward comes in the cognitive gains that can be made.

The same idea of work is something underrepresented in the stories themselves, particularly those depicting human enhancement and cognitive/consciousness extension.[4] While the science indicates that new neural capabilities need to be effortfully trained, often in fiction enhancements are given for free to fictional characters who are capable of instantly harnessing them. This seems to me to be a (fictional) leap too far. The lesson from neuroscience is that enhancements require adaptation through deliberate practice and also that specialisation in one area of cognitive growth may mean reduction of another. Here, Egan's divergent posthuman Fleshers segregated into specialism-based clans seem more believable.[5]

---

4   Exceptions that come to mind include Paolini's *To Sleep in a Sea of Stars*, where Kira trains over a long period to harness her alien skin suit. Christopher Paolini, *To Sleep in a Sea of Stars* (Basingstoke, UK: Tor Books, 2020).

5   Egan, Greg. *Diaspora* (London: Millennium, 1997).

Reality v possibility

We have repeatedly seen how inspiration from biology has informed and inspired SF authors writing about sentience and consciousness. Whether this is individual mammals, social insects, cephalopods or bacteria, whenever new knowledge is created about life on earth, it can inspire new fiction. And this can include, of course, knowledge of the human brain, human societies and aspects of group dynamics and empathy. If this tradition of following the science continues, it should be assumed that speculation will continue to be built on new cores of truth and hence constantly renewed. It also implies that authors should continue to follow new theories of consciousness and forms of experience across the known natural world.

While science makes discoveries at a steady rate, technology seems to escalate and the SF genre no longer has exclusive or even innovation rights over grand visions as to how technology will be incorporated into society.[6] But this is not important for writing about the future of consciousness. Indeed, it can be the smaller, subtle and socio-technical details that we neglect in our rush to innovate our technology that will continue to provide a useful ground for SF authors and wider fiction. Contemporary books like *Klara and the Sun*, for example, show how much needs to be thought through as we try to create artificial life to fulfil social roles.[7]

Empathy, ecological and alternative consciousnesses

Clearly, authors need great empathy to extend their own experience to alien, artificial and extended minds. What we see in more recent SF subgenres such as solarpunk, is empathy extended to our own or to imagined ecological and natural systems.[8] Once again, this is a great

---

6   As Peter Watts has pointed out, even the idea of the singularity may become irrelevant to SF in the near future if it fails to arise, or even if it *does* arrive and we move on up. Patrick, and William Lexner, 'Pat's Fantasy Hotlist: Peter Watts Interview', *Pat's Fantasy Hotlist* (blog), 22 December 2006. https://fantasyhotlist. blogspot.com/2006/12/peter-watts-interview.html.

7   Kazuo Ishiguro, *Klara and the Sun* (London: Faber and Faber, 2021).

8   Reina-Rozo, Juan David, 'Art, Energy and Technology: The Solarpunk Movement', *International Journal of Engineering, Social Justice, and Peace* 8, no. 1 (5 March 2021): 47–60. https://doi.org/10.24908/ijesjp.v8i1.14292.

opportunity for more first person or psychonarrative accounts. And there are some pioneering attempts, such in 'Whale Snows Down', the short story by Kim Bo-Young,[9] which imagines the impact of human ecosystem destruction on a community of deep-sea creatures.

N.K. Jemisin provides an innovative approach to depicting this kind of expanded consciousness in the *Broken Earth* series, showing how a psychological connection Earth's own structures can be used to both destroy and heal. The precariousness of human existence in the face of gigantic geological forces is balanced only by the specific orogenic powers of the narrator and her kin. Jemisin's portrayal of instances of orogeny feel like an expanded and repurposed empathy, with the characters having an acute understanding of exactly where tectonic pressure points are and how they can be released without causing damage.

Decentered and non-anthropomorphic fiction can also be another route to understanding how AI or aliens may conceive of their own consciousness. As Valente and numerous others have pointed out, if something claims consciousness, what right does this have to be denied? Elefsis points this out in *Silently and Very Fast*: 'What I want to say is that there is no difference between her body producing oxytocin and adrenaline and learning to associate this with pair-bonding, and my core receiving synthetic equivalents and hard-coding them to the physical behaviours I performed.'[10]

Stories such as *Silently* and Yamamoto's *The Stories of Ibis* provide first person accounts of how AI might experience analogues of human-claimed feelings of affection, loneliness and humour.[11] These stories can be informative to discussions around AI ethics, which itself has something of a fictional foundation in Asimov's 1950 laws of robotics.[12]

In considering human-AI psychological relationships, it need not be the case that there is a clear division or divergent evolution. In Stross's *Accelerando*, human-computer coupling is taken to a natural (though

---

9   Kim Bo-Young, 'Whale Snows Down', trans. Sophie Bowman, *Future Science Fiction Digest*, January 6, 2021. https://future-sf.com/fiction/whale-snows-down/.

10 Catherynne M Valente, *Silently and Very Fast* (N.p.: Wyrm, 2011).

11 Hiroshi Yamamoto, *The Stories of Ibis* (San Francisco: VIZ Media, 2010).

12 As one of Ibis's characters point out, these laws need revision, as it is impossible for a robot to prevent humans from doing foolish things to themselves! Ibid.

perhaps rather dystopic) conclusion.[13] In *Silently and Very Fast*, it is humans who fail the AI's Turing test. AIs diverge hugely from humans and leave the Earth. But it is the unique human/AI construct Elefsis which combines the two and becomes something greater.

Loops and spirals

Elefsis's power and enormous intelligence comes from the development of a shared language and a history of training spanning several human generations: 'I programmed myself to respond to Ceno. She programmed herself to respond to me. We ran our code on each other. She was my compiler, I was hers. It was a process of interiority, circling inward toward each other.'[14]

Starting with Calvino's snail, we can see loop and spiral patterns throughout our tour of fictional consciousnesses. This is not surprising given that, in a range of theories about consciousness, the brain's massive feedback and recursion features play a part in a possible root of sentience. Such looping provides a possible mechanism but is also the rock on which many accounts remain stranded. This is famously down to the inability of logic and rationality alone to avoid paradox, as Peter Watts' character despairs in *Blindsight*: 'Gödel was right after all. No system can fully understand itself.'[15]

Fiction can help us bridge this explanatory gap. Our examples have progressed through individuation, purpose and connection to future evolution, all of which phenomena have been bolstered by forms of spiralling feedback.

Toward transparency

To summarise their work exploring alien and posthuman psychology, authors have all steered a course between two shores: the inexpressible and the overly familiar. In doing so they have often navigated via a strong understanding of the biologically possible. They have identified and

---

13   Charles Stross, *Accelerando* (London: Orbit, 2005).
14   Valente, *Silently*.
15   Watts, *Blindsight*.

tried to subvert the more established fictional alien and AI motivations and behaviours.

Success at rendering non-human conscious awakenings, alien and artificial minds, hive and distributed minds has relied on some narrative stylistic choices as well as a deliberate decentering from their own subjective experience. In some cases this is supported by a spareness of detail that makes the reader work to construct a somewhat comprehensible picture of the external/fictional world and characters. In others, a relatively comfortable telling with nonetheless jolting subject matter recalls Forster's observation that fantasy and magic can be invoked through simple words.

The author's challenge is different and, in many regards, more difficult than simply writing about other humans in ways that make characters' mental states accessible to the reader—itself a huge task. What I've hoped to show through the examples in this book is the possibility of unlocking wonder and a stimulating loss of groundedness by imagining alien mental states and promoting them through the choice of language, metaphor and narrative voice.

Bibliography

Adams, John Joseph, and David Barr Kirtley. 'Interview: Vernor Vinge', *Lightspeed Magazine*, May 2012. https://www.lightspeedmagazine.com/nonfiction/interview-vernor-vinge/.

Aldiss, Brian. 'Cognitive Ability and the Light Bulb', *Nature* 403 (January 2000): 253. https://doi.org/10.1038/35002217.

Aldiss, Brian W. *Hothouse*. London: Four Square Books, 1964.

Allardice, Lisa. 'Kazuo Ishiguro: 'AI, Gene-Editing, Big Data... I Worry We Are Not in Control of These Things Any More'', *The Guardian*, February 20, 2021. https://www.theguardian.com/books/2021/feb/20/kazuo-ishiguro-klara-and-the-sun-interview.

'Ann Leckie on Ancillary Justice', *Orbit Books*, 2013. https://www.orbitbooks.net/interview/ann-leckie-ancillary-justice/.

Atwood, Margaret. *Oryx and Crake*. Toronto: McClelland & Stewart, 2003.

'Author Interview: Adrian Tchaikovsky', *The Book in Hand* (blog). May 26, 2021. https://thebookinhand.com/2021/05/26/author-interview-adrian-tchaikovsky/

Baldwin, Thomas, ed. *Maurice Merleau-Ponty: Basic Writings*. London: Routledge, 2003. https://doi.org/10.4324/9780203502532.

Baxter, Stephen. *Coalescent*. Destiny's Children Book One. London: Gollancz, 2003.

Birch, Jonathan, Simona Ginsburg, and Eva Jablonka. 2020. 'Unlimited Associative Learning and the Origins of Consciousness: A Primer and Some Predictions', *Biology and Philosophy* 35, no. 6 (2020): 56. https://doi.org/10.1007/s10539-020-09772-0.

Blackmore, Susan J. 2005. *Conversations on Consciousness*. Oxford: University Press.

Bodard, Aliette de. *The Tea Master and the Detective*. N.p.: JABberwocky Literary Agency, Inc, 2019.

Bokkon, Istvan, József Vas, Noemi Csaszar-Nagy, and Tünde Lukács. 2013. 'Challenges to Free Will: Transgenerational Epigenetic Information,

Unconscious Processes, and Vanishing Twin Syndrome', *Reviews in the Neurosciences* 25 (November): 1–13. https://doi.org/10.1515/revneuro-2013-0036.

Bo-Young, Kim. 'Whale Snows Down', Translated by Sophie Bowman. *Future Science Fiction Digest,* January 6, 2021. https://future-sf.com/fiction/whale-snows-down/.

Broderick, Damien. 'New Wave and Backwash: 1960–1980', In *The Cambridge Companion to Science Fiction.,* edited by Edward James and Farah Mendlesohn, 48–63. Cambridge University Press, 2003

Brooks, Rodney A. 1990. 'Elephants Don't Play Chess', *Robotics and Autonomous Systems* 6, nos. 1–2 (June 1990): 3–15.

Calvino, Italo. 'The Spiral', In *Cosmicomics,* translated by William Weaver. 141–53. London: Picador, 1993.

Carney, James. 'The Space Between Your Ears: Construal Level Theory, Cognitive Science and Science Fiction', In *Cognitive Literary Science: Dialogues Between Literature and Cognition,* edited by Michael Burke and Emily Troscianko, 73–92. Oxford University Press, 2017.

Chambers, Becky. *A Closed and Common Orbit.* Wayfarers 2. London: Hodder & Stoughton, 2016.

—. *The Long Way to a Small, Angry Planet.* London: Hodder & Stoughton, 2015.

Changeux, Jean-Pierre. 'Climbing Brain Levels of Organisation from Genes to Consciousness'. *Trends in Cognitive Sciences* 21, no. 3 (1 March 2017): 168–81. https://doi.org/10.1016/j.tics.2017.01.004.

Chemero, Anthony. *Radical Embodied Cognitive Science.* Cambridge, MA: MIT Press, 2009.

Chiang, Ted. *Exhalation.* London: Picador, 2019.

—. *The Lifestyle of Software Objects.* City: Publisher, 2019.

—. 'Understand', In *Stories of Your Life and Others.* London: Picador, 2014.

Clarke, Arthur C. *Childhood's End.* Reprints edition. London: Pan Books, 1953.

—. *Profiles of the Future.* London: Pan Books, 1964.

Cleeremans, Axel, Dalila Achoui, Arnaud Beauny, Lars Keuninckx, Jean-Remy Martin, Santiago Muñoz-Moldes, Laurène Vuillaume, and Adélaïde de Heering. 'Learning to Be Conscious'. *Trends in Cognitive Sciences* 24, no. 2 (1 February 2020): 112–23. https://doi.org/10.1016/j.tics.2019.11.011.

Cohen, Jack, and Ian Stewart. *What Does a Martian Look Like?: The Science of Extraterrestrial Life.* London: Ebury Press, 2004.

Cohn, Dorrit. *Transparent Minds: Narrative Modes for Presenting Consciousness in Fiction.* Princeton, NJ: Princeton University Press, 1978.

Cole, David. 'The Chinese Room Argument', in The Stanford Encyclopedia of Philosophy, edited by Edward N. Zalta and Uri Nodelman, Summer 2023. Metaphysics Research Lab, Stanford University, 2023. https://plato.stanford.edu/archives/sum2023/entries/chinese-room/.

Colzato, Lorenza S., Bernhard Hommel, and Christian Beste. 2021. 'The Downsides of Cognitive Enhancement', *The Neuroscientist* 27 (4): 322–30. https://doi.org/10.1177/1073858420945971.

Cruse, D. Alan, and William Croft, eds. 'Metaphor', in *Cognitive Linguistics*, 193–222. Cambridge Textbooks in Linguistics. Cambridge: Cambridge University Press, 2004. https://doi.org/10.1017/CBO9780511803864.009.

Davis, Philip. *Reading and the Reader*. The Literary Agenda. Oxford: University Press, 2013.

Dresler, Martin, Anders Sandberg, Christoph Bublitz, Kathrin Ohla, Carlos Trenado, Aleksandra Mroczko-Wąsowicz, Simone Kühn, and Dimitris Repantis. 'Hacking the Brain: Dimensions of Cognitive Enhancement'. *ACS Chemical Neuroscience 10*, no. 3 (20 March 2019): 1137–148. https://doi.org/10.1021/acschemneuro.8b00571.

Dunbar, R. I. M., and Susanne Shultz. 2007. 'Evolution in the Social Brain', *Science* 317 (5843): 1344–347. https://doi.org/10.1126/science.1145463.

Eagleman, David. 2020. *Livewired: The Inside Story of the Ever-Changing Brain*. Edinburgh: Canongate.

Egan, Greg. *Diaspora*. London: Millennium, 1995.

—',Interview by Carlos Pavón', By Carlos Pavón. 1998. https://www.gregegan.net/INTERVIEWS/Interviews.html.

—. 'Learning to Be Me', In *Axiomatic*, 201–20. London: Millennium, 1995.

EnJoe, Toh. 'Overdrive', In *Self-Reference ENGINE*. Translated by Terry Gallagher. San Francisco: Haikasoru/ VIZ Media, 2016.

Fauconnier, Gilles, and Mark Turner. *The Way We Think: Conceptual Blending And The Mind's Hidden Complexities*. Reprint ed. New York: Basic Books, 2003.

Forster, E M. *Aspects of the Novel*. [Pelican Books. no. A557]. Harmondsworth: Penguin Books, 1962.

Foster, Alan Dean. *Nor Crystal Tears*. New York: Del Rey, 1982.

Fronhofer, Emanuel A., Jürgen Liebig, Oliver Mitesser, and Hans Joachim Poethke. 'Eusociality Outcompetes Egalitarian and Solitary Strategies when Resources are Limited and Reproduction is Costly'. *Ecology and Evolution 8*, no. 24 (2018): 12953–2964. https://doi.org/10.1002/ece3.4737.

Fujii, Taiyo, Toh EnJoe, and Tobi Hirotaka. 2016. *Saiensu Fikushon 2016*. Haikasoru.

George Lakoff. 2003. *Metaphors We Live by*. Metaphors We Live by/George Lakoff and Mark Johnson. Chicago, Ill.; London: University of Chicago Press.

Gibson, William. 'The Afterword Reading Society: The Peripheral by William Gibson', Culture. *The National Post*, December 10, 2014. https://nationalpost.com/entertainment/books/the-afterword-reading-society-the-peripheral-by-william-gibson.

—. *Neuromancer*. New York: Ace, 1984.

—. *The Peripheral*. London: Viking, 2014.

Glendinning, Simon. *In the Name of Phenomenology*. London: Routledge, 2006.

Godfrey-Smith, Peter. *Other Minds: The Octopus, the Sea and the Deep Origins of Consciousness*. EPub edition. London: William Collins, 2017.

Goff, Philip, William Seager, and Sean Allen-Hermanson. 2022. 'Panpsychism', in *The Stanford Encyclopedia of Philosophy*, edited by Edward N. Zalta, Summer 2022. Metaphysics Research Lab, Stanford University. https://plato.stanford.edu/archives/sum2022/entries/panpsychism/.

Grau, Carles, Romuald Ginhoux, Alejandro Riera, Thanh Lam Nguyen, Hubert Chauvat, Michel Berg, Julià L. Amengual, Alvaro Pascual-Leone, and Giulio Ruffini. 2014. 'Conscious Brain-to-Brain Communication in Humans Using Non-Invasive Technologies', *PLOS ONE* 9 (8): e105225. https://doi.org/10.1371/journal.pone.0105225.

Hayles, N. Katherine. *How We Became Posthuman: Virtual Bodies in Cybernetics, Literature, and Informatics*. Chicago: University of Chicago Press, 1999.

Hofstadter, Douglas R. 2001. 'Analogy as the Core of Cognition', *Stanford Presidential Lectures in the Humanities and Arts*, 42.

Hölldobler, B., and Edward O. Wilson. *The Superorganism—The Beauty, Elegance and Strangeness of Insect Societies*. Illustrated edition. New York: W. W. Norton & Co., 2009.

Hoyle, Fred. *The Black Cloud*. London: Heinemann, 1958.

Hughes, David P., and Frederic Libersat. 2019. 'Parasite Manipulation of Host Behavior', *Current Biology* 29 (2): R45–47. https://doi.org/10.1016/j.cub.2018.12.001.

Hutchins, Edwin. 2020. 'The Distributed Cognition Perspective on Human Interaction', In *Roots of Human Sociality*, edited by N. J. Enfield and Stephen C. Levinson, First, 375–98. Routledge. https://doi.org/10.4324/9781003135517-19.

Iser, Wolfgang. *The Act of Reading: A Theory of Aesthetic Response*. Baltimore; London: The John Hopkins University Press, 1978.

Ishiguro, Kazuo. *Klara and the Sun*. London: Faber & Faber, 2021.

Jemisin, N.K. *The Obelisk Gate*. London: Orbit, 2016.

Johnson, Andrea. 'Interview: Greg Egan on Orthoganal and Thirty Years of Writing Hard Science Fiction'. SF Signal (blog), 6 June 2014.

https://www.sfsignal.com/archives/2014/06/interview-greg-egan-on-orthogonal-and-thirty-years-of-writing-hard-science-fiction/.

Jones, Gwyneth A. *White Queen*. New ed. New York: Orb Books, 1994.

Keyes, Daniel. *Flowers For Algernon*. New edition. London: Cassell, 1966.

Kirk, Robert. 'Zombies', in *The Stanford Encyclopedia of Philosophy*, edited by Edward N. Zalta and Uri Nodelman, Summer 2023. Metaphysics Research Lab, Stanford University, 2023. https://plato.stanford.edu/archives/sum2023/entries/zombies/.

Koch, Christof. *The Feeling of Life Itself: Why Consciousness Is Widespread but Can't Be Computed* (Cambridge, MA: The MIT Press, 2019)

Kross, Karin L. 'William Gibson on Urbanism, Science Fiction, and Why *The Peripheral* Weirded Him Out', *Tor.com*, October 29, 2014. https://www.tor.com/2014/10/29/william-gibson-the-peripheral-interview/.

Krznaric, Roman. 2014. *Empathy: A Handbook for Revolution*. London: Rider Books.

Lakoff, George. *Metaphors We Live By*. Chicago, Ill. ; London: University of Chicago Press, 2003.

Le Guin, Ursula K. *Late in the Day: Poems, 2010–2014*. Oakland, CA: PM Press, 2016.

—. *The Left Hand of Darkness*. New York: Time Warner International, 1987.

Lea, Richard. Science Fiction: The Realism of the 21st Century', *The Guardian*, August 7, 2015. https://www.theguardian.com/books/2015/aug/07/science-fiction-realism-kim-stanley-robinson-alistair-reynolds-ann-leckie-interview?CMP=share_btn_tw.

Leckie, Ann. *Ancillary Justice*. London: Orbit, 2013.

—.*Ancillary Mercy*. London: Orbit, 2015.

Lem, Stanisław. 'The Mask', In *Mortal Engines*, 181–239. London: Penguin Classics, 2016.

—. *Solaris*. Berkley Publishing Corporation, 1971.

Lessing, Doris. *Shikasta: Re: Colonised Planet 5: Personal, Psychological, Historical Documents Relating to Visit by Johor (George Sherban) Emissary (Grade 9) 87th of the Last Period of the Last Days/Doris Lessing*. Lessing, Doris, 1919–2013. Canopus in Argos: Archives 1. London: Flamingo, 1994.

—. 'A Thing of Temperament: An Interview with Doris Lessing, London, May 16, 1998', By Cathleen Rountree, *Jung Journal* 2, no. 1 (2008): 62–77. https://doi.org/10.1525/jung.2008.2.1.62.

Lewin, Sarah. 'Alien Minds, Alien Tech (and Spiders, Too): Q&A With Sci-Fi Author Adrian Tchaikovsky', *Space.com*, May 15, 2019. https://www.space.com/children-of-ruin-adrian-tchaikovsky.html.

Liberman, Nira, and Yaacov Trope. 2014. 'Traversing Psychological Distance', *Trends in Cognitive Sciences* 18 (7): 364–69. https://doi.org/10.1016/j.tics.2014.03.001.

Lodge, David. *Consciousness and the Novel: Connected Essays*. Cambridge, Mass.: Harvard University Press, 2002.

Manaugh, Geoff. 'Unsolving the City: An Interview with China Miéville', *BLDGBLOG*. March 1, 2011. https://www.bldgblog.com/2011/03/unsolving-the-city-an-interview-with-china-mieville/.

Marshall, Brooks E., and this link will open in a new window Link to external site. 2020. 'The Disenchanted Self: Anthropological Notes on Existential Distress and Ontological Insecurity Among Ex-Mormons in Utah', *Culture, Medicine and Psychiatry* 44 (2): 193–213. https://doi.org/http://dx.doi.org/10.1007/s11013-019-09646-5.

McCaffrey, Anne. *The Ship Who Sang*. London: Rapp and Whiting Ltd, 1971.

Merleau-Ponty, Maurice. *Maurice Merleau-Ponty: Basic Writings*. London: Routledge, 2003.

Miéville, China.*Perdido Street Station*. London: Tor Books, 2008.

Minsky, Marvin. *The Society of Mind*. New York: Simon & Schuster, 1986.

Morgan, Dan. *The Several Minds*. London: Corgi Books, 1969.

Naam, Ramez. *Nexus*. Nottingham, UK: Angry Robot, 2013.

Nagel, Thomas. 1974. 'What Is It Like to Be a Bat?' *The Philosophical Review* 83 (4): 435. https://doi.org/10.2307/2183914.

Nam, Chang S., Zachary Traylor, Mengyue Chen, Xiaoning Jiang, Wuwei Feng, and Pratik Yashvant Chhatbar. 2021. 'Direct Communication Between Brains: A Systematic PRISMA Review of Brain-To-Brain Interface', *Frontiers in Neurorobotics* 15. https://doi.org/10.3389/fnbot.2021.656943.

Natassia. 'Interview: Ramez Naam | Literary Escapism', 12 September 2013. https://www.literaryescapism.com/39192/interview-ramez-naam.

Navarrete, Ana F., Simon M. Reader, Sally E. Street, Andrew Whalen, and Kevin N. Laland. 2016. 'The Coevolution of Innovation and Technical Intelligence in Primates', *Philosophical Transactions of the Royal Society B: Biological Sciences* 371 (1690): 20150186. https://doi.org/10.1098/rstb.2015.0186.

Nelles, William. 'Austen's Juvenilia and the Sciences of Mind', In *Jane Austen and Sciences of the Mind*, edited by Beth Lau, 1st edition, 14–36. Routledge, 2017.

Oatley, Keith. *Such Stuff as Dreams: The Psychology of Fiction*. Chichester, West Sussex, UK: Wiley, 2011.

Orhanen, Anna. n.d. 'An Exclusive Q&A with Kazuo Ishiguro on Klara and the Sun', *Waterstones.com Blog*. https://www.waterstones.com/blog/an-exclusive-qanda-with-kazuo-ishiguro-on-klara-and-the-sun.

Otto, Rudolf. 1923. *The Idea of the Holy*. Oxford: Oxford University Press.

Pagan, Nicholas. 2014. *Theory of Mind and Science Fiction*. Palgrave. https://doi.org/10.1057/9781137399120.0001.

Paolini, Christopher. *To Sleep in a Sea of Stars*. Basingstoke: Tor Books, 2020.

Perrakis, Phyllis Sternberg. 'The Marriage of Inner and Outer Space in Doris Lessing's 'Shikasta''. *Science Fiction Studies* 17, no. 2 (1990): 221–38.

Poirier, Pierre, and Guillaume Chicoisne. 2006. 'A Framework for Thinking about Distributed Cognition', *Pragmatics & Cognition* 14 (2): 215–34. https://doi.org/10.1075/pc.14.2.04poi.

Poulet, Georges. 1969. 'Phenomenology of Reading', *New Literary History* 1 (1): 53–68. https://doi.org/10.2307/468372.

Powers, Richard. *Galatea 2.2*. New York: Picador USA, 2004.

—. *Bewilderment*. New York: W.W. Norton, 2021. Kindle. Vintage Digital.

Reynolds, Alastair, Nnedi Okorafor, Ann Leckie, Becky Chambers, Kim Stanley Robinson, and M. John Harrison. "If the Aliens Lay Eggs, How Does That Affect Architecture?': Sci-Fi Writers on How They Build Their Worlds', *The Guardian*, January 5, 2021. https://www.theguardian.com/books/2021/jan/05/if-the-aliens-lay-eggs-how-does-that-affect-architecture-sci-fi-writers-on-how-they-build-their-worlds.

Richardson, Alan. 2014. 'Imagination: Literary and Cognitive Intersections', In *The Oxford Handbook of Cognitive Literary Studies*, edited by Zunshine, Lisa. Oxford University Press.

Roberts, Adam Charles. 2016. *The History of Science Fiction*. Palgrave Histories of Literature. London: Palgrave Macmillan, 2016.

Robinson, Kim Stanley. *Aurora*. London: Orbit, 2016.

Robson, David. 'When Did Consciousness Evolve?' *New Scientist* 250, no. 3342 (July 2021): 39. https://doi.org/10.1016/S0262-4079(21)01205-7.

Robson, Justina. 'Dreadnought', *Nature* 434 (March 2005): 680. https://rdcu.be/dbhSt.

Rock, Irvin, and Stephen Palmer. 1990. 'The Legacy of Gestalt Psychology', *Scientific American* 263 (6): 84–90. https://doi.org/10.1038/scientificamerican1290-84.

Rucker, Rudy B. *Software*. New York: Ace Books, 1982.

Scalzi, John. 'The Big Idea: N.K. Jemisin', *Whatever: Furiously Reasonable* (blog), August 6, 2015. https://whatever.scalzi.com/2015/08/06/the-big-idea-n-k-jemisin-4/.

Scott, Veronica. 'Interview with Martha Wells, Author of The Murderbot Diaries', Science Fiction. *Amazing Stories,* July 27, 2018. https://amazingstories.com/2018/07/interview-with-martha-wells-author-of-the-murderbot-diaries/.

Seth, Anil. 2021. *Being You: A New Science of Consciousness*. Main edition. London: Faber & Faber.

Shamay-tsoory, Simone G. 2019. 'Herding Brains: A Core Neural Mechanism for Social Alignment', *Trends in Cognitive Sciences* xx: 1–25. https://doi.org/10.1016/j.tics.2019.01.002.

Shelley, Mary Wollstonecraft. *Frankenstein, or, The Modern Prometheus*. Longman Cultural Edition. 2nd ed. Edited by Susan J. Wolfson. New York: Pearson Longman, 2007.

Shvartsman, Alex. 2020. *Future Science Fiction Digest Volume 9: The East Asia Special Issue*. Independent.

Silverberg, Robert. *Dying Inside*. London: Sidgwick and Jackson, 1974.

Skinner, B. F. "Superstition' in the Pigeon'. *Journal of Experimental Psychology* 38, no. 2 (1948): 168–72. https://doi.org/10.1037/h0055873

Smith, E. E. *The Galaxy Primes*. St. Albans, UK: Panther Books, 1975.

Solms, Mark, and Jaak Panksepp. 2012. 'The 'Id' Knows More Than the 'Ego' Admits: Neuropsychoanalytic and Primal Consciousness Perspectives on the Interface Between Affective and Cognitive Neuroscience', *Brain Sciences* 2 (2): 147–75. https://doi.org/10.3390/brainsci2020147.

Stapledon, Olaf. *Star Maker*. Penguin Science Fiction. London: Penguin Books, 1937.

Stross, Charles. *Accelerando*. London: Orbit, 2005.

—. 2013. *Neptune's Brood*. Orbit.

Sturgeon, Theodore. 'The Push From Within: The Extrapolative Ability of Theodore Sturgeon', Interview by David D. Duncan, *Emory University*. http://www.physics.emory.edu/faculty/weeks//misc/duncan.html.

—. *More Than Human*. New York: Farrar, Straus, & Young, 1953.

Suvin, Darko. *Metamorphoses of Science Fiction: On the Poetics and History of a Literary Genre*. New Haven, CT: Yale University Press, 1979.

Swirski, Peter. 2000. *Between Literature and Science: Poe, Lem, and Explorations in Aesthetics, Cognitive Science, and Literary Knowledge*. Montreal; London: McGill-Queen's University Press.

Swirsky, Rachel. 'Grand Jeté (The Great Leap)', *Subterranean*, Summer 2014.

Taylor, Dennis E. *We Are Legion (We Are Bob)*. 2nd ed. New York: Ethan Ellenberg Literary Agency, 2017.

Tchaikovsky, Adrian. *Children of Ruin*. London: Tor Books, 2019.

—. *Children of Time*. London: Tor Books, 2019.

Turner, Mark. *The Literary Mind: The Origins of Thought and Language*. New York: Oxford University Press, 1996.

Valente, Catherynne. *Silently and Very Fast*. Wyrm, 2011.

VanderMeer, Jeff. "God, That's a Merciless Question': China Miéville's Interview From Weird Tales', *Jeff VanderMeer* (blog). June 16, 2009. https://www.jeffvandermeer.com/2009/06/16/god-thats-a-merciless-question-china-mievilles-interview-from-weird-tales/.

—. *Annihilation*. The Southern Reach Trilogy. London: Fourth Estate, 2014.

Vinge, Vernor. *A Fire Upon the Deep*. London: Millennium, 1992.

Watts, Peter. *Blindsight*. London: Tor Books, 2006.

—. 'Peter Watts Interview', *Pat's Fantasy Hotlist* (blog), December 22, 2006. http://fantasyhotlist.blogspot.com/2006/12/peter-watts-interview.html.

—. 'The Things', *Clarkesworld Magazine*, January, 2010. no. 40. https://clarkesworldmagazine.com/watts_01_10/

Weisz, Erika, Desmond C. Ong, Ryan W. Carlson, and Jamil Zaki. 2020. 'Building Empathy Through Motivation-Based Interventions', *Emotion*, November. https://doi.org/10.1037/emo0000929.

Wheeler, Michael. 'Martin Heidegger', in *The Stanford Encyclopedia of Philosophy*, edited by Edward N. Zalta, Fall 2020. Metaphysics Research Lab, Stanford University. https://plato.stanford.edu/archives/fall2020/entries/heidegger/.

Whiten, Andrew, Christine A Caldwell, and Alex Mesoudi. 'Cultural Diffusion in Humans and Other Animals'. *Current Opinion in Psychology*, Culture, 8 (1 April 2016): 15–21. https://doi.org/10.1016/j.copsyc.2015.09.002.

Wickham, Kim. 2019. 'Identity, Memory, Slavery: Second-Person Narration in N. K. Jemisin's 'The Broken Earth Trilogy'', *Journal of the Fantastic in the Arts* 30 (3): 392–411, 479.

Yama, Hiroshi, and Norhayati Zakaria. 'Explanations for Cultural Differences in Thinking: Easterners' Dialectical Thinking and Westerners' Linear Thinking'. *Journal of Cognitive Psychology* 31, no. 4 (19 May 2019): 487–506. https://doi.org/10.1080/20445911.2019.1626862

Yamamoto, Hiroshi. 'AI's Story', In *The Stories of Ibis*, translated by Takami Nieda. San Francisco: VIZ Media, 2010.

—. 'Black Hole Diver', In *The Stories of Ibis*, translated by Takami Nieda (San Francisco: VIZ Media, 2010).

Young, Kay. 2010. *Imagining Minds: The Neuro-aesthetics of Austen, Eliot, and Hardy*. Theory and Interpretation of Narrative Series. Columbus: Ohio State University Press.

Zelazny, Roger. ''Kjwalll'kje'k'koothaïlll'kje'k', In *An Exaltation of Stars: Transcendental Adventures in Science Fiction*, edited by Terry Carr. New York: Pocket Books, 1974.

—. 'Zelazny & Amber—Phlog44 RZ Interview', Interview by Alex Heatley. 1995. http://www.roger-zelazny.com/repository/phlogiston_interview.html.

Index

About the Team

Alessandra Tosi was the managing editor for this book.

Elisabeth Pitts performed the copy-editing and proofreading. The index was created by Rosalyn Sword.

Jeevanjot Kaur Nagpal designed the cover. The cover was produced in InDesign using the Fontin font.

Melissa Purkiss typeset the book in InDesign and produced the paperback and hardback editions. The text font is Tex Gyre Pagella; the heading font is Californian FB.

Cameron Craig produced the EPUB, PDF, HTML, and XML editions. The conversion was made with open-source software such as pandoc (https://pandoc.org/), created by John MacFarlane, and other tools freely available on our GitHub page (https://github.com/OpenBookPublishers).

This book has been anonymously peer-reviewed by experts in their field. We thank them for their invaluable help.

This book need not end here...

Share

All our books — including the one you have just read — are free to access online so that students, researchers and members of the public who can't afford a printed edition will have access to the same ideas. This title will be accessed online by hundreds of readers each month across the globe: why not share the link so that someone you know is one of them?

This book and additional content is available at:

https://doi.org/10.11647/OBP.0348

Donate

Open Book Publishers is an award-winning, scholar-led, not-for-profit press making knowledge freely available one book at a time. We don't charge authors to publish with us: instead, our work is supported by our library members and by donations from people who believe that research shouldn't be locked behind paywalls.

Why not join them in freeing knowledge by supporting us:

https://www.openbookpublishers.com/support-us

Follow @OpenBookPublish

Read more at the Open Book Publishers **BLOG**

You may also be interested in:

Life, Re-Scaled
The Biological Imagination in Twenty-First-Century
Literature and Performance
Liliane Campos and Pierre-Louis Patoine (eds)

https://doi.org/10.11647/OBP.0303

Technology, Media Literacy, and the Human Subject
A Posthuman Approach
Richard S. Lewis

https://doi.org/10.11647/OBP.0253

Zombies in Western Culture
A Twenty-First Century Crisis
John Vervaeke, Filip Miscevic and Christopher Mastropietro

https://doi.org/10.11647/OBP.0113

This book need not end here...

Share

All our books — including the one you have just read — are free to access online so that students, researchers and members of the public who can't afford a printed edition will have access to the same ideas. This title will be accessed online by hundreds of readers each month across the globe: why not share the link so that someone you know is one of them?

This book and additional content is available at:

https://doi.org/10.11647/OBP.0348

Donate

Open Book Publishers is an award-winning, scholar-led, not-for-profit press making knowledge freely available one book at a time. We don't charge authors to publish with us: instead, our work is supported by our library members and by donations from people who believe that research shouldn't be locked behind paywalls.

Why not join them in freeing knowledge by supporting us:

https://www.openbookpublishers.com/support-us

Follow @OpenBookPublish

Read more at the Open Book Publishers **BLOG**

You may also be interested in:

Life, Re-Scaled
The Biological Imagination in Twenty-First-Century Literature and Performance
Liliane Campos and Pierre-Louis Patoine (eds)

https://doi.org/10.11647/OBP.0303

Technology, Media Literacy, and the Human Subject
A Posthuman Approach
Richard S. Lewis

https://doi.org/10.11647/OBP.0253

Zombies in Western Culture
A Twenty-First Century Crisis
John Vervaeke, Filip Miscevic and Christopher Mastropietro

https://doi.org/10.11647/OBP.0113